GOLD STAR SISTER

"Gram, Gram. Come in here. I found this neat old trunk."

"Oh, my Lord. Dad's old steamer trunk. I'd forgotten all about it."

"Open it, Gram."

"My father brought this trunk with him when he moved to America. Everything he owned was in this trunk."

Finally she opened the lid.

A light gray shoe box with a red ribbon tied around it was tucked way down in one corner. I noticed there was writing on the box—the name "Billy" in dark blue crayon.

Later I couldn't stop thinking about the box. Who was Billy? Could Gram's memory be that bad? No, Gram knew. So why did she want to keep it a secret?

"Readers looking for a fresh spin on World War II fiction [will] find the tale enjoyable."

—*Bulletin of the Center for Children's Books*

OTHER PUFFIN BOOKS YOU MAY ENJOY

Barry's Sister Lois Metzger
Beat the Turtle Drum Constance C. Greene
Colt Nancy Springer
Did You Hear about Amber? Cherie Bennett
Forever Friends Candy Dawson Boyd
Life's a Funny Proposition, Horatio Barbara Garland Polikoff
Listen for the Fig Tree Sharon Bell Mathis
Little By Little Jean Little
Love You, Soldier Amy Hest
Phoenix Rising Karen Hesse

CLAIRE RUDOLF MURPHY

Gold Star Sister

PUFFIN BOOKS

PUFFIN BOOKS
Published by the Penguin Group
Penguin Books USA Inc., 375 Hudson Street, New York, New York 10014, U.S.A.
Penguin Books Ltd, 27 Wrights Lane, London W8 5TZ, England
Penguin Books Australia Ltd, Ringwood, Victoria, Australia
Penguin Books Canada Ltd, 10 Alcorn Avenue, Toronto, Ontario, Canada M4V 3B2
Penguin Books (N.Z.) Ltd, 182-190 Wairau Road, Auckland 10, New Zealand

Penguin Books Ltd, Registered Offices: Harmondsworth, Middlesex, England

First published in the United States of America by Lodestar Books, an affiliate of
Dutton Children's Books, a division of Penguin Books USA Inc., 1994
Published in Puffin Books, 1996

1 3 5 7 9 10 8 6 4 2

THE LIBRARY OF CONGRESS HAS CATALOGED THE LODESTAR EDITION AS FOLLOWS:
Murphy, Claire Rudolf.
Gold star sister / by Claire Rudolf Murphy—1st ed. p. cm.
Summary: While watching her grandmother cope with the last stages of cancer,
thirteen-year-old Carrie comes to know her better through letters Gram
and her long-dead brother wrote to each other during World War II.
ISBN 0-525-67492-6
[1. Grandmothers—Fiction. 2. Cancer—Fiction. 3. Death—Fiction.
4. World War, 1939–1945—Fiction.] I. Title.
PZ7.M9525Go 1994
[Fic]—dc20 93–48135 CIP AC

Puffin Books ISBN 0-14-037744-1

Printed in the United States of America

to my mother-in-law, Ann Murphy, with love,
and in memory of
Marilyn Bowder and Irene Wickwire

ACKNOWLEDGMENTS

Thanks to veterans Mervin Bishop and Ed Beistline, Sandy Connelley, Ann Murphy, and my parents Fran and Kerm Rudolf, for sharing their memories of World War II; nurse Claudia Anderson, Tara Heery, and Jean Turner, for information on cancer; Father Andrew Maddox of Immaculate Conception Church, Nancy Schmidt of the United States Postal Service, the public information service at Fort Wainwright, my editor Virginia Buckley, my agent Liza Voges, and my family.

Thanks also to the seventh grade reading students of Bob Murphy and Carl Addington at Ryan Middle School, who responded to *Gold Star Sister* as a work-in-progress.

Gold Star Sister

Chapter One

"GRAM, I'M HERE. Gram? Where are you?" Throwing my backpack on a chair, I take off my shoes. Gram's pretty protective about her wood floors.

I love this house. Gram says it has character—so many little rooms and closets on all three floors, from the basement to the attic. Not like our new house, where everything's small and smashed together on one floor.

My sisters and I used to play hide-and-seek here for hours. Once when Lisa was it, she couldn't find Molly for a long time. So she finally gave up and we started playing dolls. After a while, when Molly still didn't appear, we looked again and found her curled in a ball in the basement, crying.

"You dumbo," Lisa said. "Why didn't you just come out and yell 'Olly, olly, oxen free.' "

"Because you have to be found. That's the rules." That's our Molly, always playing by the rules.

"In here, Carrie."

I walk down the hallways, stopping to look at the picture of Dad as a kid. I always laugh when I see it. He's about four years old and has a big frown on his face, probably because he's wearing this silly jacket and shorts with his chubby little legs sticking out.

So that's where I got them. The chubby O'Leary legs.

Thanks, Dad. Aunt Rosemary is holding his hand and smiling. But she has slim legs and so does Gram. What happened to me?

"Carrie, I'm in your grandfather's room." My nose scrunches up, ready for the musty smell. But the windows are all open and Gram is sitting on the floor, folding shirts and putting them in a box.

Until today Gram has left Gramps's room the way it was on the day he died. Even though it was kind of creepy, I enjoyed going in there; it made me feel closer to him, like any second he might get up from his desk, a pipe in hand and wearing his favorite red wool shirt. He used to squeeze me hard, never letting go until I did.

"Hi, Gram. What are you doing?"

"Clearing out your grandfather's things. About time, wouldn't you say?"

Right before Christmas, Dad and Gram got into a big fight about Gramps's things. Gram said since he was her husband, she would get rid of them when she was good and ready. But Dad said six months was long enough

I open the closet and see his ugly printed ties. That's what Gram always called them. Gramps would nod, then put one on anyway.

I stoop down and take one of his leather shoes off the shoe rack. It's hardly been worn. Gramps didn't like to dress up much, though Gram never stopped trying to make him.

"Say, would the drama department at your school like some of these clothes?"

"I don't know." I put the shoe back. "Gram, why are you moving in with us? Don't get me wrong. I'm happy about it. But you love this house. If you're lonely, I could come and live with you here."

"Carrie, honey, your family would miss you." Fat chance. "And without your grandfather around, this place is just too big for me. I have to admit that for once your father is right. I need a smaller place." Gram grabs the desk chair as she struggles to get up.

"Gram, let me help you. Are you all right?"

"Oh, these old bones are just getting tired, I guess." Gram never used to talk like this. Last summer she played tennis three times a week, and I hardly ever beat her.

She walks over to the closet and takes the ties off the rack. "Just as soon as those darn chemotherapy sessions are over, I'm going to find myself a condominium."

"But, Gram, they're so small."

"Hush. No sense talking about it now. The house is sold, and soon a new family will live here." I look around, tears in my eyes. Gram's eyes stay dry.

"You know, I could use a break," she says, leading me out of the room. "This is our last chance for milk and cookies in my kitchen." I start laughing.

"Oh, excuse me. A little old for that, are we?" Gram sticks out her hand, then points toward me with her chin and, speaking in her best English accent, says, "Carrie, darling, would you care to join me for tea?"

"Why, I would love to, Ann, dear."

Gram doesn't act sick. She looks so young, with her clear white skin and slim body. Her hair is gray now, but it's a pretty gray—not bluish like those old ladies in hairnets.

"Isn't this your last day of school? I thought you'd be busy celebrating with your friends."

Shaking my head, I finish my second cookie. "We don't get out until Tuesday. Besides, I don't have any friends now that Sally's gone."

Gram moves the cookie plate toward me. I push it away. "No, thanks. I've got to lose weight. It's bathing suit weather."

"Carrie, you look just fine." Gram stares at me. "Say. I like your new haircut. Those bangs show off your green eyes," Gram says, pouring herself another cup of herbal tea. She's been on a health kick since they discovered breast cancer in January.

"I quit softball yesterday," I say, grabbing another of Gram's irresistible oatmeal/chocolate chip cookies.

"Carrie, I thought you loved softball."

"Everybody knows I stink. I think the coach was secretly relieved."

"Sounds like we're feeling a wee bit sorry for ourselves today."

"Well, you would be, too, if you had my life. Ms. Chambers handed back our World War II papers today. I got a big fat C, which probably means I'll get a C in the class, too."

"What happened to your straight A's?"

"Gram, that was sixth grade. As Mom puts it, I've had a little trouble adjusting to middle school."

"So tell me more about this report." Gram takes our cups over to the sink and immediately starts washing them. She can never just sit still.

"Well, I suppose I'm lucky I even got a C since it was only half done. It could have been an A. I know it. But no, I had to skip school with that stupid Nancy, who only asked me because she had a test that day and nobody else was around. Anyway, it all added up to two weeks of detention, which bummed me out so much that I put off everything, including this report, until the day before it was due."

Gram goes into the dining room and starts taking her Waterford crystal out of the china closet and wrapping it in newspaper. I follow and sit on the floor next to her. Gram holds up a glass. "Remember. This is the Carrie pattern. It will be yours someday." I nod. How could I forget?

"We had to interview somebody who had lived during World War II. By then, you were in Washington, D.C., on your trip, and Mom and Dad wouldn't let me call Grandma and Grandpa Collins long distance because Dad said there were plenty of people right in town I could interview for free."

"So *who* did you end up interviewing?" Gram always sounds like she's really interested in what I'm doing, not like Mom, who's usually half listening while she does something else, or Dad, who acts like he hasn't heard a word I said.

"Mr. Kingston down the block. I'm going to fix you up with him." I raise my eyebrows at Gram in a knowing look. "I used to think he was weird, but it was fun talking to him."

"You will do no such thing. Besides, you're right. He always was somewhat odd."

"Well, he's not. Anyway, by then I was desperate."

"So what did he say?"

"He really got into it. He brought out all his medals and pictures and even a diary he wasn't supposed to keep because of security reasons. He served in the North Pacific theater in Alaska. I didn't know they fought World War II in Alaska. In fact, when I told Dad, he made me look it up in the encyclopedia just to be sure. Of course, Mr. Kingston was right. The Japanese invaded some islands up there, the uh . . ."

"The Aleutians."

"Yeah, that's right. Anyway, Mr. K fought on Attu when they tried to get the island back from the Japanese. But it turns out the Japanese had snuck away in boats during the night before the Allies landed. Spooky, huh?"

Gram is staring out her big picture window. "Gram? Hello . . . Gram?"

Her face is white, like she has just seen a ghost or something. Gram finishes wrapping the glass in her hand and puts it in the box.

"You better go lie down, Gram. You don't look so good."

"Don't be silly. Go on with your story," she says, trying to smile.

"Well, that's about it. Except that Mr. K had to go out to dinner, so he invited me to come back another day to hear more about the war and look at his stuff. But I got busy this week, and today he left on a trip in his camper."

"Alone?"

"No, he went with his new girl friend." I nudge Gram. "But I don't think he's that serious about her. Maybe it's not too late to get in on the action."

Gram pushes up her nose and seems like her old self again. She hates camping. What she thinks about Mr. Kingston, I'm not sure.

Gram puts her hand over mine. "You sound like you learned a great deal, Carrie."

"All the good it did me. Mr. K said it's really beautiful up there with all the glaciers and mountains and wild animals. I'd like to visit Alaska sometime. That is, if I have anyone to go with."

Gram stands up and takes another piece of newspaper off the table.

"Oh, here I go again. Boring you with all my problems when you have enough of your—"

"Carrie Ann O'Leary, you are not boring me and never have," Gram says, waving the newspaper at me. I grab it out of her hand and run into the living room. She follows me, yelling, "And as for me, this so-called cancer is not a problem. A mere bump on the highway of life."

More like a lump or many lumps, I think, balling up the newspaper and tossing it into the wastebasket.

It's all so crazy. Gram with lumps, me with bumps, Lisa with humps, and Molly with pumps in her arms. I start laughing.

"What's so funny?" Gram says, grabbing me and giving me a hug. I hug her back, then pull her down on the couch with me.

"Gram, why don't *we* take a trip together? Next month when your treatments are over."

"I don't know."

"But now you won't have the house or lawn to worry about . . ."

"Now that you mention it, your grandfather and I always planned to take you girls to San Francisco and show you where I grew up. But between our summers at the lake and then your grandfather's illness . . ."

"So let's go now."

Gram looks at me and smiles. "Yes, you and your sisters. And maybe Tom, too."

My cousin Tom? He'd ruin everything. I start pacing the living room. "Well, if they're too busy to come, you and I can take the dog together."

"Dog?"

"Greyhound. That's what Sally always calls it. She wrote and told me that I should take the dog to come visit her in Vermont."

"Yes. I'd like that, Carrie. We'll ride the dog to San Francisco."

I like the idea, too. Lisa and Molly would never lower themselves to ride a Greyhound bus all the way to California. Good. I'll have Gram all to myself.

Chapter Two

SATURDAY MORNING—Gram's moving in today. I can't wait. I wake up early because there's so much to do. But Molly still hasn't cleared out my half of the room, and she's at swim practice. So I go down to the kitchen for breakfast. Opening the cupboard, I pull out the Shredded Wheat, determined to stick to my diet. I don't care what Gram says. Good-bye, O'Leary thighs.

Molly, the eleven-year-old swim star, saunters in from her

morning workout just as I pour my cereal. "Dried grass for breakfast, Carrie? How delicious."

"Yes, sister dear, I feel outdoorsy today. What's it for you? Another Hershey bar after swim practice?"

"Jealous?"

Of course I'm jealous, I think, slamming the box down on the table. She's got a million friends; fourteen-year-old boys on the swim team are in love with her; and to top it off, she always makes the honor roll.

I pull back my long, straight hair and pour some milk into my bowl. I can almost hear Molly snicker. She's already spritzed and ditzed her dark, curly hair to perfection, even though in a few short hours she'll be back in the pool.

"No, Lisa Look-Alike. But you could move your stuff so I can move in. Have you forgotten that Gram's coming today?"

"How could I, with all your ranting and raving? And for your information, I'm not like Lisa. I'm my own person. You think you're so special just because you have red hair."

For better or for worse, my hair is the one feature other girls seem to notice. Actually, I'm sick of people telling me I have the thickest, reddest hair they've ever seen. Besides, it's not red. It's auburn. I look over at Molly. Could she actually be envious of my hair?

"I want things to be nice for Gram, that's all."

"Well, so do I."

"Then clear out half the room for me."

"Would you mind if I had a little breakfast first?"

Dad walks in, holding a piece of paper. "Carrie, guess what came in the mail?" How could I have missed the mailman? He never comes this early.

"What, Dad?" I hold my breath and pray.

"Your report card. All C's. I see that nothing's changed, even though you promised it would. I can't believe it belongs to the same girl who got straight A's in sixth grade."

"I really tried this quarter, Dad. I thought I was bringing my grades up, but then—"

"You got detention for skipping school," Molly finished happily.

"Shut up, Molly."

"Carrie, you know we don't like those words used in this house."

"Well, it's none of her business, Dad."

"No, it isn't. It's yours, mine, and your mother's. And we've decided to ground you for two weeks."

"But Dad—"

"No more discussion. I'm off to get your grandmother. Hopefully, she'll have more patience with you."

Molly sits smirking as Lisa comes in, wearing her pink bathrobe, high-heel slippers, and red lipstick. Who in their right mind wears lipstick before breakfast?

I storm around making toast, wondering how I'm going to get out of being grounded. Maybe I could just drive everybody crazy and they'd have to let me leave the house. Oh, where would I go, anyway?

"So what was that all about?"

"Dad grounded Carrie for her horrible grades."

"Carrie, look on the bright side," Lisa says, leaning against the doorway. "I think it's good to work against type sometimes. Take me, for instance. I don't always want to look dressed up when I go out on errands. Sometimes it's good for people to see that I can look great in just jeans and a T-shirt."

I want to throw up, especially when she goes over to the little mirror by the sink and starts studying her teeth. Finally she turns around and asks, "Do my teeth look yellow? Maybe I should try some of that tooth whitener I've seen advertised." Molly and I look at each other and burst out laughing.

"Okay. Okay. So it's a dumb idea. Nobody's ever accused

me of being brilliant. But today's my first day at Nordstrom's, and I don't want to make a fool of myself."

She walks to the table and takes a bite out of my toast. "Hey, that's my toast," I say, grabbing it back.

"But I thought you were on a diet." Then she makes a face. "Carrie, did you put butter on it? I cannot afford any more fat." I get up and start to leave the kitchen.

"I'm sorry, Carrie," Lisa says, grabbing my arm and bringing me back in. "Look. You were the smart and responsible one in elementary school. Now you're just proving you can be stupid sometimes, too." Lisa sits down next to me and takes my other piece of toast.

"Thank you, Lisa. That is so helpful," I say, grabbing my second piece of toast out of her hand. "You are the stupid one. You got all C's, too. So why didn't Dad ground you?"

Lisa stands up. "Because Dad knows that I'm the dumb one of the family. Do you have to rub it in?" She leaves the room in a huff while Molly stares at me.

"Couldn't you have at least helped me out, Miss Straight A O'Leary?"

"Carrie, when you open your mouth, nobody can help you."

I slam out of the kitchen and go to my old room to pack up the rest of my things. How am I going to survive Molly? She's such a know-it-all. And the walls are so thin around here that Gram and I will never have a chance to talk in private.

Twenty minutes later Molly is still in the kitchen eating. How somebody that skinny can eat so much I'll never know. I used to be able to eat four pieces of toast at a time, too. I still can. But now it shows because as Mom says, I'm becoming a woman. Well, if that's what it means, I don't want any part of it.

Finally I go back to the kitchen. "Molly, do you think you

could interrupt your feeding schedule for just a few minutes? Gram's going to be here any time."

Molly looks up calmly. No eleven-year-old deserves to be this calm. "Carrie, I am not an elephant in the zoo. I am a growing girl." She takes one last bite of her toast, then slowly loads her dishes in the dishwasher while I stand there waiting. She never loads her dishes when Mom asks her to.

"Beat you to my room," she yells, as she sprints past me, a victory smile on her face.

I arrive in the bedroom and fall on her bed, panting. I look up, and from the ceiling Olympic swim star Janet Evens smiles down at me, four gold medals hanging around her neck. "Don't forget, sis," she says, sweeping her small, muscular arms around her, "this room is still *mine*. You're just staying in here until—"

"Until what?" I sit up. "Until Gram dies or something? You are so selfish."

"No. You are so *morbid*. Gram isn't going to die. She just has breast cancer."

"Molly's right," Lisa says, strutting into the room like a model on a runway. Lord, take me away from these women. "I read somewhere that half the women in America have breast cancer or will someday get it, and they're not all dying."

"Since when are you two medical authorities? You barely passed biology, Lisa. And you don't even *have* breasts, Molly." Why did I say that? Molly has bigger breasts than I do, even if that's not saying much.

I start making the second bed in Molly's room with the sheets Mom left, talking all the while, hoping they didn't hear what I just said. "Plenty of women have died from breast cancer. And even if they do remove all the cancer, like they say they did with Gram, she's not considered cured unless no new cancer appears for at least five years. *And* did you know that breast cancer is inherited?"

Lisa and Molly look at each other.

"Personally, I think she's getting worse and they're all just keeping it a secret. Why else would she sell her house and move in here?"

"It did all happen pretty fast," Molly says.

"Oh, lighten up, would you guys?" Lisa goes over to the dresser and starts combing her hair.

"Easy for you to say, Lisa. You're not the one who has to share a room, who's grounded for two weeks, who has no friends."

"Girls, girls." Mom walks in, looking tired but still pretty. Why didn't I get her clear, dark skin instead of freckles? "What would your grandmother think? Come on. Everybody grab some of Carrie's boxes and bring them in here." She looks around the room. "Molly, you haven't even finished arranging the room for Carrie."

"I know, Mom. But I've been so busy with the extra swim practices and final tests at school and—"

"Enough of the excuses. Just get it done."

"Mom, why *is* Gram moving in with us? She really loved her old house." Molly grabs Mom's arm. "Is Gram going to die? And are we going to get breast cancer, too?"

"Molly, honey. Women make full recoveries from breast cancer all the time. We'll talk about this later. But right now we have to get Carrie's room ready for your grandmother."

At the doorway Mom stops and looks at us. "Molly, Carrie is moving into your room, like it or not. So you're both going to have to make the best of it."

Lisa goes over and hugs Mom. "Don't worry, Mom. They will. I'll see to it." Mom smiles and then leads us into my old room, where she starts handing us boxes.

"Mom, I'm sorry, but I can't help right now. I'm already dressed for work." Lisa twirls around. "Do I look too fat in these white pants?"

"You look wonderful, honey."

"But I'm not sure what jacket to wear. Could you come help me decide?"

Mom nods and we all follow Lisa into her room. She holds up the first jacket for Mom and then notices us. "Out, out, you two," she yells, pushing us toward the door. "You're tramping all over my new white carpet. Molly, come back and take that box off my clean white bedspread."

"Don't blame me. I was just following Carrie."

I drop my box on the floor and scream, "I've had it. I get blamed for everything around here. I'm the one giving up my room. Has anybody considered that?"

"What would your grandmother think of all this?" Dad asks, standing in the doorway.

I run over to him. "Is she here yet, Dad?"

"No, thank goodness. She had a few last-minute things she wanted to do at the house, so I brought a load over here first."

"Will, *what* is your mother doing at the house?"

Dad shrugs. "Probably cleaning the bathroom one more time."

"She never listens to what I say. She knows that the cleaning service is coming in Monday to do all that. She shouldn't be working in her condition."

Dad goes over and puts his arm around Mom. "I know this has been rough on you. But it's her last day in the house. She should get to do whatever she wants. There will be plenty of time for her to rest here. That is, if there isn't any more fighting."

"Come on, Molly, let's finish moving the boxes," I say, wanting to get out of the room as quickly as possible.

"Bye, everybody. I don't want to be late."

"Lisa, aren't you going to be here when your grandmother arrives?"

"But, Dad, it's my first day at Nordstrom's, remember?"

"What time is it?" Molly yells out.

"Noon," Lisa says, looking at her new watch.

"I almost forgot. Coach called a special team meeting for twelve-thirty. Can you drop me off at the pool, Lisa? I'll have to do extra laps if I'm late."

"Sure. But grab your stuff. We've got to leave right now."

"Wait a minute. Wait a minute," Dad says, grabbing their shoulders as they start out the door. "I thought we were all going to have lunch with Gram on her first day here."

"Lunch? Will, you never mentioned anything about lunch. We don't even have her room ready yet."

"Molly, you can't leave yet. You haven't finished clearing out my half of the room, and then we have to help Mom get Gram's room ready."

"Oh, just throw the stuff on my side. I'll put it away later."

"No, your sister's right, Molly. You can't go until you've finished the job."

"But Mom, *I have to go*. Coach won't let me race next Saturday if I miss the meeting."

Dad throws up his hands and sits on Lisa's bed. "All right. All right. I give up. But dinner's here at six P.M.—no excuses." Lisa and Molly nod and run out the door.

Some things never change. One more time my sisters get out of doing work and instead go forth into the world to find more glory. Meanwhile, Carrie the Drudge stays home cleaning the house. Just like Cinderella—except in my version, the sisters are pretty and Cinderella has no fairy godmother.

Wait a minute. Gram's my fairy godmother. And as soon as she's through with chemo, we're going to blow this cookie joint and head for California. Who said the fun has to end at midnight?

Chapter Three

DAD AND I SPEND THE NEXT HALF HOUR moving my things into Molly's room, while Mom cleans out my old one. When we're finished, I beg Dad to let me drive over to Gram's with him, to see her house one last time.

"I grounded her this morning, Susan."

Mom stops washing the windows and looks at Dad. "I don't think a trip to your mother's counts, and I know she'd appreciate having Carrie along."

Then Mom looks over at me. "I know this is hard on you, honey, giving up a room and all."

"No. I'd do anything to help Gram get better. Anything," I say, running out of the room.

Driving down the street, Dad doesn't say a word. Just hums along to some sixties song on the radio. Finally, I say, "Dad, is Gram going to die? Is that why she's moving in with us?"

We come to a red light, and Dad slams on the brakes. "Carrie, where did you get such an idea?"

"But she doesn't look good, Dad. I thought she was doing better, but when I stayed with her last weekend, she was tired all the time and her bones were hurting and—"

Dad grips the steering wheel. "The chemo treatments are hard on her. Besides she's sixty-nine and lives alone. She just needs our help, that's all."

That's the trouble with my dad. He either ignores me or doesn't level with me. But I don't care. Today's my lucky day. Gram's moving in.

"You must be kind of sad about it, Dad."

"Sad?" He looks over at me. "Because of your grades? No,

more like disappointed, because I know you can do much better than that."

For two hours now I had forgotten about my report card. But thanks to Dad, it was going to be a long summer.

"No, about Gram's house. Pretty soon a new family will move in and fill it up with their memories."

"Hey, I'm the one who grew up in the house. So why are you getting so sentimental?"

"Dad, you know what I mean. All those secret things hidden in the basement and attic."

"Oh, Carrie of the curious mind." He laughs.

"Well, you can learn a lot from history. I'm going to major in it in college." Dad laughs again. "That is, if my grades improve." Why don't I just keep my stupid mouth shut?

Secrets. I stare out the window at the rain. Then I start to write my name on the foggy window, but my hand starts spelling out "Billy" instead. Billy. Oh, my god. I'd forgotten all about him. Forgotten all about last Saturday in Gram's basement.

We had stayed up late watching *Gone With the Wind*. Gram's favorite movie. We gave her the video last Christmas. As usual, Gram fell asleep in the middle of it. But not me. I won't close my eyes until I hear Rhett's last line, "Frankly, my dear, I don't give a damn." Usually Gram's awake to tell me how scandalous the word *damn* was in those days.

The next morning Gram made me her delicious pancakes. I told her that Mr. Kingston had invited me to come over sometime for sourdough pancakes from his starter, which had originated with some Alaskan gold miners almost a hundred years ago. She just sniffed at me.

Then I told her that since we didn't have a garden, she could help Mr. Kingston with his, but she just ignored me. Said we should get busy packing before she got too tired.

I followed Gram down the wooden steps into the basement. Molly, Lisa, and I used to play dress-up for hours down there in Gram's old clothes. Lisa and Molly should have come for one last overnight. No date or swim practice is that important. I guess some things will never be the same again.

Boxes were piled everywhere. "Where did all these come from?" I asked Gram.

"Everybody's junk just kept accumulating, and I've got to sort through it all before the movers come next week. Your small house can't possibly hold all this."

Gram pointed toward a pile, and the first box I opened was a bunch of old clothes. I pulled out the sweater on top and held it up to me—the Irish knit sweater Gram had made me.

"Gram, I didn't know you had saved this for me. I remember you made it for my eighth birthday. I loved it so much and was so sad when I couldn't wear it anymore. Remember when I wore it on Easter Sunday the next year and Lisa said I looked like a stuffed rabbit? She made me so mad. I was still really skinny then. She was just jealous because she wasn't anymore."

"I seem to remember some words between the two of you." Gram started walking around, opening up more boxes.

"Words. Huh. We got into this huge fight right before we went out for Easter brunch, and I ran to my room crying. Gramps came upstairs and found me. I told him I didn't want to grow up—that I wanted to stay the same age forever."

"What did he say, honey?" Gram stopped and looked at me.

"He said he felt the same way sometimes, but that other times he couldn't wait to get older." I put the sweater back into the box. "Gram, I didn't think grown-ups ever wanted to get older. Do you?"

"Oh, yes, Carrie. I want to get as old as I can."

Neither of us spoke for a moment. "Do you still really miss him, Gram?"

"There will always be a hole in my heart, honey. But people like you help fill it up. Carrie, look." Gram motioned me over to a box of old blue dishes from the cabin at Priest Lake.

I picked up a plate and pretended to see my reflection. Me in my lumpy blue bathing suit with wet, stringy hair. Then I started to shiver.

Gram put her arms around me. "You kids would stay in your suits all day, swimming off the dock."

"Then around four o'clock you would walk down to the dock and sneak us some money to go buy candy at the resort store."

"You never told your parents, did you?"

"Gram, don't you think they wondered where we got the money?"

Gram started laughing. I love to hear her laugh. And it makes her face look healthier.

"I miss going to the cabin, Gram."

"So do I, honey."

I heard Gram and Dad talking in the den one day last year around the time Dad's roofing company was having financial problems. A few days after that, Dad told us the cabin was up for sale, but then never mentioned it again. It was Gram who told me that the Jacksons down the beach had bought it for their grandchildren. Lucky them.

She just said it matter-of-factly, with no feeling at all. Was she upset and just covered it up so Dad wouldn't feel guilty? Like she covered up her cancer for a while before telling us? Gram and Gramps had built the cabin a year after they were married. How can you let go of something like that and not be sad?

And to top it off, Dad's company went under anyway, and he had to go to work for somebody else. Since then, nobody has dared talk about the cabin. Except Lisa, who forgot the other day and brought it up when we were talking about summer plans. Dad didn't say anything, as usual.

After a while, I wandered into the toolroom, where there were even more boxes. Way back in one corner I spotted a big trunk I'd never seen before.

I walked over to it, shoving boxes out of my way as I went. When I reached the trunk, I saw that it was covered in canvas with brown wooden trim and had a lock that was broken.

I lifted the lid, then quickly put it down. I really wanted to see what was inside, but knew I'd better ask first.

"Gram, Gram. Come in here. I found this neat old trunk."

I figured I was going to have to drag her away from what she was doing, but then there she was, staring at it.

"Oh, my Lord. Dad's old steamer trunk. I'd forgotten all about it." Gram ran her hand along the lid.

"Open it, Gram."

"My father brought this trunk with him when he moved from County Donegal to America. Everything he owned was in this trunk."

"When was that, Gram?"

"Around 1919, I think. Soon after World War I."

I was dying to see what was inside, but I pressed my lips together so I wouldn't ask again. Gram hates it when I push her too hard.

Finally she opened the lid. The inside was covered with red-flowered wallpaper and had a wooden shelf sitting on top. Gram touched the empty shelf, then lifted it out. Underneath were several small cardboard boxes.

"Well, which one first?" I said, but Gram wasn't listening.

"Oh, Carrie. It's been such a long time since I've looked in this trunk." She pulled out a box and studied the outside. "Look at this. Beemer Jams. I used to make boxes like this at their factory."

"You did?"

"I certainly did. During the war all the ammunition factories were recruiting workers, but my father wouldn't allow me to take a job, especially since I was still in high school. Finally I talked him into letting me work at Beemer Jams during the summer." Gram studied the box again.

"We all had different jobs. Some of the girls put labels on the jars; others helped make the jam. And some of us made boxes. See how it's stapled here."

She turned the box over and showed me. "We'd just take an unfolded box, put it together, then staple it, click, click, click. Some days I would be assigned to paint on the design with a stencil. Pretty nifty, huh?"

I stared at Gram, trying to picture her as a teenager, working in a jam factory.

Gram opened the box, but it just had some old sewing notions. While Gram looked at them, I searched around the trunk. A light gray shoe box with a red ribbon tied around it was tucked way down in one corner. It was the ribbon that drew my attention.

When I pulled it out, I noticed there was writing on the box—the name "Billy" in dark blue crayon. In the Palmer method, the perfectly looped writing that Gram says the nuns taught her at St. Cecilia's.

"This looks like your handwriting, Gram."

Gram grabbed the box from me and studied it.

"Is it?" I asked. She finally nodded.

"Then who's Billy?"

Gram shrugged her shoulders and put the box carefully down on the floor.

"Was he a relative, Gram?"

Gram still didn't answer—just took out another box and opened it. "Look, Carrie. My old dolls." Gram held one up. "Oh, Shirley Temple. Mother gave this to me on my ninth birthday; and here's Sonja Henie. She won three Olympic gold medals in figure skating, you know."

I tried to look at the dolls and listen to what she was

saying, but I kept thinking about the gray box. It was small, and fairly lightweight, so there couldn't be much in there. Letters, maybe? Yeah, letters to Gram from Billy. But who was Billy?

When we went back upstairs, Gram took the Billy box with her. "When are you going to open that box, Gram?" She smiled and kept on walking. "When you do, I guess you'll find out who Billy is."

"I guess so," she said, carrying it into her bedroom.

Later I couldn't stop thinking about the box. Who was Billy? Could Gram's memory be that bad? No, Gram knew. So why did she want to keep it a secret? Maybe Billy was an old boyfriend, a man she loved before Gramps.

But Gram said it was her dad's trunk. Was her dad's name Billy? No, it was Gram's handwriting. And she wouldn't call her dad Billy, would she?

Turning onto Gram's street, I suddenly remember to ask Dad about it. "Is there a relative in the family named Billy?"

"Me."

"Dad, you've always been Will. You were never called Billy, were you?"

"Sure. Mom used to call me that. But when I got into school, I wanted to be called Will because I thought it sounded more grown-up."

"Oh."

"Why the questions?"

"I just heard Gram mention a Billy once and I wondered who it was."

"It could have been me. But she hasn't called me that since I was a kid. But you know your grandmother. She knows the whole world, so it could be anybody." For being Mr. Closemouthed, Dad sure was into this conversation. "If you're so interested, why don't you ask her?"

If only it were that simple, I think, getting out of the car. But maybe it *is* Dad's stuff. His baby pictures or something.

Then why wouldn't Gram show them to me? What's so secret about baby pictures?

No, I don't think it's Dad's stuff. It's something bigger than that. Maybe she's already looked through the box and is going to show it to me tonight.

Gram doesn't waste a minute getting into the car, saying she doesn't want to drag out her farewell to the house. She won't even let me walk through the house one last time.

Then, as Dad drives away, Gram takes the Shirley Temple doll out of her purse and says, "Didn't you forget something last weekend?"

"Thanks, Gram. I was just going to ask you about the dolls."

"Let's show them to your sisters. Tonight at dinner."

Great, I think. And you'll probably tell them all about Billy, too—after I was the one who discovered him.

Chapter Four

HERE I WAS, looking forward to having Gram around, but right after lunch she takes a nap. Says I can help her unpack later. So I go back to the kitchen and look around for something to eat. I'm still hungry. Opening a package of graham crackers, I think about bodies. Is it better to be skinny and have no breasts or a little chubbier *with* breasts? And what about me—chubby with no breasts? I'm really unbalanced.

I wonder if Gram had breasts when she was my age. If she did, it doesn't matter now. When she first got cancer, she told me she wished that she had smaller breasts, so that maybe the cancer cells would have gone right by without seeing them.

Did Gram open the Billy box? Is she going to tell me tonight who Billy is?

Mom and Dad come into the kitchen, and Mom frowns when she sees the graham crackers. Isn't she ever hungry?

"While your grandmother is napping, we thought we'd go out on a few errands. Please answer the phone and doorbell quickly so they don't wake her."

I nod. We never had to protect Gram before.

What am I supposed to do now? I can't leave the house. I just finished reading *Anne of Green Gables* for the twentieth time last night. My parents don't believe in Nintendo. No soaps on Saturday. I guess I could finish arranging my stuff. But then I notice the doll box sitting on the kitchen counter, so I take it to Molly's—I mean *our*—room. Molly has been so selfish about this whole thing.

Mom tried to cheer Molly up by telling her it would be good experience for college. But Molly said she was sure to end up with a better roommate than me. Then she suggested that maybe I should move in with Lisa because we were closer to college age and would need the experience sooner.

Maybe I would be better off rooming with Lisa. No, all her clothes and makeup are everywhere. And I have a better shot at bossing Molly around. She *is* two years younger, even though she tries to act like eleven going on twenty.

I stop outside Lisa's door. Holding the doll box in one hand, I gently turn the knob and tiptoe in. How would I like to live in here? Ugh. White rug, white dressing table, white curtains with just a hint of pink on the ruffle.

Prissy, tissy, that's my sister. Modeling classes since she was twelve and now a teen fashion consultant. How boring—always having to be beautiful and tell others they look wonderful in whatever clothes they try on at the store.

I walk over to the three-way mirror. Lisa worked on Mom for a whole year to buy this thing. Eventually Mom gave in, like she does on everything involving Lisa or Molly. And now every morning Mom's in here, too, checking to see how *she* looks from every angle.

I look worse than I feel. How is that possible? I turn back to the white dressing table: everything lined up just so, even the contact case containing the new lenses Lisa got last week. She'd been working on Mom and Dad to buy those, too. Finally she asked them, "Have you ever seen a model with glasses?" That's when Dad said he would loan her the money and she could pay it back from her earnings.

I start to pick up the contact case when the doorbell rings. I put it down and run out of the room. What if Lisa caught me in here? She'd kill me. I lie down on Molly's bed, my heart pounding.

Then I sit up. Lisa wouldn't ring the doorbell. Who is ringing the doorbell? I do not want to see anyone. Where is Molly when I need her?

Ring. Ring. I go into Mom and Dad's room and hide behind the curtains on the window facing the front yard. *Ring. Ring.* If you wait long enough, the person will come out on the sidewalk and you can find out who it is without answering the door. Then if you want to see the person, you've still got time to dash to the front door. Ever since we moved in, it's been our secret place to spy on people in the neighborhood.

The doorbell rings again, and then I remember Gram. If that dumb bell has waked Gram up, I'm going to . . . Where is my brain? I start to leave, but the ringing stops and someone comes off the porch.

Fatty Maddie. Waddling down the sidewalk. What is she doing here? I haven't hung out with her in ages. We don't even talk at the bus stop anymore.

Phew. She's gone. I can see her swaying all the way back to her house. Gram's block has so many trees you wouldn't be able to watch anyone, but not our block. Most of the trees were cut down, and the houses are all crammed together.

I walk down the hallway and listen at Gram's door, but she doesn't seem to be up.

Fatty Maddie, I think, going back to Molly's room and sitting on my bed. Mom would say, "Carrie, that's not nice." And it isn't nice. But she is fat. I mean *really* fat. But nobody calls her Fatty Maddie to her face anymore because she'd beat you up if you did.

We kinda used to be friends until Sally moved in behind us and Mad got so mean. She wasn't quite as fat then. Mom and Patty—that's what Mad's mom always wants me to call her—used to drive around looking at houses on Sundays. I never could figure out why they were friends, and now it seems they're not. Patty wears kind of radical clothes—flowered skirts and Birkenstock sandals—and has frizzy, permed hair. She works at an art gallery.

Mom works at a bank. She used to be a potter. But when Dad's business went under, Mom had to find a job that paid real money. She wears business suits with little bow ties. I am never going to dress like that.

We kids only went on the house tours because we got ice cream afterward. Licorice. That was Mad's favorite. I liked peppermint back then. Now it's mint chocolate chip all the way.

I liked it better when Lisa and Molly didn't come. If they did, all four of us would be jammed in the backseat, fighting. And Maddie would always end up biting somebody, usually Molly.

Sometimes Gram would come along, too, and Gramps would stay home and watch baseball games with Dad. Mad's never had a dad around. I guess he took off when she was a baby and never showed up again.

That would be weird. Even though my dad hardly talks, at least he's still around, and maybe he'll even start relating to me more before I graduate from high school, especially if my grades improve.

I don't hate Mad, I think, staring out at the green lawn I was supposed to mow. I kind of admire her, actually. She's not afraid of anything or anybody.

The phone rings. I run out into the hall and grab it on the second ring. "Hello."

"Carrie Ann"—all the neighbors still call me that even though I *hate* it—"I just came over to your house and nobody answered the door. Did you hear the doorbell ring?"

"No." White lie, here we come.

"But I was just there. Are you sure you didn't hear it?" I can hear Mad's teeth grinding over the phone line. "Now I suppose you're going to tell me that your doorbell's broken?"

"No. But I *was* taking a nap, so I guess I didn't hear it."

"Don't you at least want to know why I came over?"

Not really. "Why did you?" It comes out kind of snotty. Gram would not be impressed with my manners.

"I came over to see your gram because she's one of the few people I really like and I heard that she's pretty sick. Is that why she's staying with you?"

"No, she's fine. It's just that the chemo treatments are hard on her sometimes."

"Oh. You know, Carrie Ann, your grandmother respects me. She's never called me fat or even hinted about diets or anything."

"I've never called you fat."

"Right. 'Fatty Maddie two by four, couldn't get through the bathroom door.' You and everybody else on the bus."

"I never said that on the bus."

"You laughed. Just like you laughed when I was slow running the bases in kick-the-can. You and your sister Molly, especially."

What is this, a counseling session? I sit on the floor.

"Oh, forget it. You're not my shrink. So can I come over or not?"

"Gram's taking a nap right now."

"But you just said she was fine."

"She is, but she's tired, like me."

"Okay. So I'll visit you."

She sure doesn't take a hint, I think, as I walk to the front door. Nobody has to know, and at least I can stop her from ringing the bell again.

Mad is wearing these baggy bloomer pants, covered with bright orange and red flowers. They make her look twice as huge. I start to say something but shut my mouth.

"So what are we going to do?" she asks, barging into the living room.

"I don't know. I thought you'd have an idea."

"But it's your house."

"But you're the one who invited yourself over here." Mad just stands there, looking at me. "Okay. Okay. I guess we could look at my gram's old dolls." Why did I say that? She's going to laugh her head off. Fine. Then maybe she'll go home.

"Great. I really like dolls."

"You do?"

"Sure. I mean, if they're really old ones. It's not like I sit around playing with Barbie dolls, if that's what you think."

The only time I ever remember Mad playing with dolls was at Molly's fifth birthday party, when she bit off the hands of Molly's birthday Barbie. I start laughing really hard.

"What's so funny?"

"These dolls. Wait until you see them," I say, opening the door to Molly's room. But then I remember I left the box on Lisa's bed.

"Wait here. I'll be right back."

I run into Lisa's room and grab the box. Turning around quickly, I bump into Mad coming in the door. "Let's get out of here."

"Why?"

"Because Lisa will have a fit if she finds out we were in here."

"Lisa, Smisha." Mad pushes past me and plops herself down on Lisa's perfectly made bed. "Does she control everything you do? I've always wanted to see what her gorgeous white room looks like."

Mad gets up and goes over to Lisa's dressing table and picks up the contact case. "When did she get these?"

"Last week. Put them down." I'm trying not to sound panicked, for then Madeline will really screw things up. She's like that.

"Carrie, darling, mustn't speak so loudly or your grandmother will wake up."

I lower my voice to the meanest whisper I have. "Put those down right now or you're never coming back to this house."

"Touchy, touchy." Mad's still holding the case in her hand.

"Fine. I guess I'll just have to get the dolls out after you go home."

She puts down the case without another word, and we go back into my room.

It's fun playing with the dolls. Besides Shirley Temple and Sonja Henie, there are five little identical dolls with matching clothes and cribs with their names on them. "I'll bet these are the Dionne quintuplets," Mad says.

"How do you know?"

In an Albert Einstein voice she says, "Don't you know I'm brilliant?"

"Right."

"It's true. They lived in Canada a long time ago and were famous all over the world because there had never been quints before."

"You're full of it. I never know when to believe you."

"I'll bet you five dollars I'm right. We'll ask your gram when she wakes up."

"You're on." We shake on it.

Then we find some paper dolls in the bottom of the box. Really sturdy ones made of heavy cardboard, not the flimsy ones like we have today. There are all kinds of them. Movie stars like Judy Garland and even a young John Wayne in a cowboy outfit.

Mad picks one up, a little girl wearing a blue dress and big yellow hat, and starts reciting:

> "In an old house in Paris that was covered with vines
> lived twelve little girls in two straight lines. . . .
> They left the house at half past nine
> in two straight lines in rain or shine—"

"What are you talking about?"

"Don't you know the Madeline stories? You know, the smallest one was Madeline and all she said was pooh, pooh, and Miss Clavel and all that."

"No," I say, shaking my head. Mad may not be school smart, but she sure knows about other things. She would break the bank on the quiz show *Jeopardy*.

"You poor deprived child. My mother has read them to me since I was in the womb. She said she always knew she would name her daughter Madeline. And she did, even though when I came out I wasn't very small."

I can't help laughing. Madeline always makes fun of herself first, before anybody else can.

She starts talking about all the other Madeline books. But I start thinking about the Billy box and how I have to find out who he is.

"Hey, yoo-hoo, Carrie. You're not listening."

"Oh, sorry. Let's go have a snack." I wish I could tell Mad about Billy. But I don't trust her yet. She'd probably barge right in and demand the box from Gram.

In the kitchen, we start munching away on some potato chips and talking about how much better the old paper dolls are than the flimsy modern ones, when Molly shows up. "Oh, hi, Matty," she says, running into the kitchen.

"Ma*dd*ie. The name's Maddie, as in Madeline."

"So sorry Matt—Dee—Line. Just didn't expect to see you around, that's all." Molly raises her eyebrows up and down at me. Then she takes a saintly lone carrot out of the refrigerator and eats it while bopping around. She's so hyperactive. No wonder she's skinny. She never stops moving.

"Oh, I'd say the Dionne quints are better than TV or swimming, wouldn't you, Carrie? Well, I'd better get going." Getting up, Madeline scrapes her chair on the floor and almost trips.

Molly starts to smirk, but before she can, Mad is in her face, glaring. Then she's at the door, smiling and waving good-bye. "Always a pleasure."

Before Molly can even ask, "What quints?" she's gone. Molly turns back to me. "What's she talking about?"

I shrug my shoulders. "You know how weird she is."

"So you're that desperate for friends now, Carrie? Tch, tch, tch," she says, munching on a chip and shaking her head. Then she picks up the sports page, probably scanning the headlines for her name. I lean over to snatch it, but she grabs my arm instead.

"Is she still as mean as she used to be? Let's check out this arm for teeth marks."

I pull my arm away. "For your information, she came over to visit Gram. She says Gram's the only nice person in this neighborhood."

"That's because Gram's the only person she's never bitten in this neighborhood," Molly yells as I push through the swinging kitchen door.

When I get to our bedroom, I throw the dolls into the box and shove it under the bed.

I'm not sharing them with Molly or Lisa. They'll probably just think the dolls are stupid. But Mad didn't. Am I desperate like Molly says?

Chapter Five

AFTER A WHILE, I go out into the hallway to see if Gram's up yet. She never used to sleep this much. *Is her cancer worse?* I'm going to make Dad tell me. Just like I'm going to make Gram tell me about Billy.

I walk over to Lisa's door. Mad's right. Why can't I look at Lisa's contacts? Since she refuses to show me, I'll just have to look at them myself. I start to touch the knob. But then I hear a car in the driveway. I tiptoe back into the dining room. Mom and Dad are unpacking groceries in the kitchen.

"Oh, Molly. I guess we forgot the milk. Would you bike to the store and get some? I want to help your dad with dinner."

Back in my parents' bedroom, I watch out the window until Molly and her bike disappear down the street.

Sneaking into Lisa's room, I check around to make sure Lisa's not hiding in a corner. Silly. She's working at Nordstrom's.

My eyes zoom in on the dressing table, then the white contact case. I walk over and stretch out my hand, but then pull it back. Lisa probably takes fingerprints on it every night.

But then my hand reaches out again, and this time I touch it. I can't help it. Just like last night when I touched the last brownie in the pan and couldn't resist eating it.

I pick up the case just to see how it feels in my hand. My eyes are perfect so I'll probably never even need glasses, let alone contacts. Two compartments marked *L* and *R*. It wouldn't hurt just to open one and see what the lenses look like.

Lisa won't even let us in the bathroom when she's putting them in. Says she needs her concentration. And she never lets me borrow any of her clothes, either, even though we're practically the same size. Well, maybe I am a little bigger.

Click. I open the *L* one. Just a teeny circle of clear plastic floating in liquid. Lisa says she doesn't need tinted lenses to show off her beautiful green eyes.

Click. I open the *R* one. Same thing. Then I hear somebody in the hallway. My body jerks. Both contacts spill on the floor into the white shag carpet and leave my hands covered with liquid.

I freeze. Who is out there and how am I going to find these stupid contacts? Trying to breathe slow, I carefully get down on my knees, expecting to hear a crunching sound any second. I search the area lightly with my fingertips. Nothing. I'm afraid to crawl around any further. What if I break one? I'll never hear the end of it. I stretch out my arms as far as I can without moving my legs.

Tears start coming down my face. Lisa's in the hall and she's going to walk in this room any minute and catch me in the act. The diary incident all over again. I broke the lock on Lisa's diary when I was eight because I wanted to read about her boyfriends. She's never forgiven me. It was Fatty Maddie's idea, but who got the blame and who's had to live with her family's distrust all these years?

I look over at the clock on Lisa's bedside table. Five-thirty. I feel around again with my fingers. Nothing.

Someone is knocking on Molly's door—"Carrie? Molly?"—then knocks on Lisa's door. "Lisa? Are you in there?" It's Gram. My whole body relaxes.

"Come in, Gram," I call out in my quietest voice, praying nobody's with her. When she opens the door, I motion with my hand for her to stop, then put my finger to my lips.

"Gram, I dropped Lisa's new contacts onto the carpet." She nods, then slowly gets down on her knees and crawls toward me, searching with her fingers as she goes. Before I know it, she's holding up one contact. I hand her the case and she puts the first one away. We both begin searching again, but Gram finds the second one, too. What would I do without her?

Gram clicks the case open and puts the second one in. "I know they have some way of marking them, but I'm not sure what."

"Gram, I'm sure they're fine. Let's get out of here."

"Wait. Hand me that bottle of contact fluid." Gram squirts some fluid in both sides. "There. Just slip this back onto Lisa's dresser and we're home free."

On the way out, I notice that Madeline has messed up Lisa's bed. "Go on, Gram. I'll be right there."

A minute later, I do feel home free, until Molly reaches the end of the hallway just as I come out of Lisa's door.

"What are you doing?"

"Shutting Lisa's door."

"Why?"

"Because it was open, silly."

"Why was it open?"

"How should I know? Maybe she left it open when you guys went out in such a hurry today."

I start to walk down the hall to Gram's room, but Molly stops me. "I think you snuck in there to borrow some of Lisa's clothes. No, I know." Molly sticks her finger right into my chest. I want to tear it off. "You were looking for another diary."

"That's ancient history, Molly, and none of your business, anyway."

"Yes, it is. I would love to keep a diary, but I don't dare with *you* around."

"Look. I don't like sharing a room any more than you do, but I'll do anything to help Gram get better."

"Why are you whispering?"

"Because Gram's right in there," I say, pointing to my old room. "Have you forgotten so soon?"

"I love Gram, too, you know. You always act like you're the only one who does." It's no use arguing with Molly.

I knock on Gram's door. "Come in." Gram is sitting in a chair by the window. "Carrie, don't you think it's—"

"I know, Gram. But Lisa won't ever let—"

"Molly, hello, dear."

Molly runs over and hugs Gram. "I'm so glad you're here, Gram." Then she looks up at me. "What are you guys talking about?"

I don't even hear what Gram says to Molly because just then I spy the gray box with the red ribbon, the Billy box, sitting right on Gram's bed. And Dad hollers out that dinner's ready.

We have already started eating when Lisa comes home from the store. She hugs Gram, then starts telling us about her first day at work.

Mom just stares at Lisa. "Why aren't you wearing the contact lenses you absolutely *had* to have for this job?" Lisa shrugs her shoulders.

Yeah, why isn't she? It sure would have saved me a lot of trouble.

"Mom, I'm just getting used to my contacts. I didn't want to spend my first day on the job fiddling around with them."

"I know what she did, Will. She wore them too long yesterday. Didn't I warn you about that, Lisa? Your Uncle Jack did that once too many times and never did get used to his."

"Susan, your brother Jack can't get used to anything, unless he's running it."

My mother glares at Dad and everybody else just eats the lasagna.

"I'll go change my clothes and be right back," Lisa says in her chirpy voice.

Soon she's back in slim, tight-fitting jeans and no glasses. "Now you're wearing nothing, Lisa?"

"Oh, I wouldn't say she's wearing nothing, Susan," Gram says, and we all start laughing.

"Mom, calm down. I put in the contacts."

"Then why are you blinking so much? Come over here, dear. Let me take a look."

I'm dead meat now. I glance over at Gram, but she's watching Lisa.

"Mom, please. Couldn't I just eat dinner? Jeff's going to be here in fifteen minutes."

"Another date? On your grandmother's first evening with us?"

"Dad."

"Hey, everybody, guess what Gram and I found in her basement last weekend?" Gram looks up, startled. Oops. Did she want to be the one to tell them?

"What?" Molly asks, jumping out of her seat. Can't she ever sit still? "You didn't tell me you found anything." Too late now. I wait to see if Gram will answer, but she doesn't.

"This box of old dolls that Gram had when she was a kid—way before World War II."

Dad starts laughing. "Well, not *way* before, Carrie."

"I always thought it would be cool to live during World War II," Lisa says, serving herself some salad. "Everybody was so patriotic and got behind the war, not like during Vietnam. And girls got to dance with soldiers at the USO and sell war bonds and everything."

I look at Lisa with amazement. I expected her to say how awful the clothes were back then or how ugly the hairstyles.

"Why, Lisa, I didn't know you were so interested in World War II," Dad says.

"We studied it in history last quarter." I look at her again. Why didn't she mention that before? She could have helped me with my report.

Dad smiles. "I agree with you, Lisa."

"You do? I thought you hated war, son."

"I do, Mother. But Lisa's right. The country *was* more united during World War II. Maybe because it was easier to figure out who the enemy was—Hitler, Mussolini, and the imperialistic Japanese."

"But it was still a war above all else." Gram puts down her fork and looks round the table. "And years without our men close to home until eventually some came back in body bags."

Nobody says anything. I start eating my salad.

"Did you lose anybody in the war, Ann?"

Gram takes a sip of water, then answers. "We all did, Susan. I'm sure your family did, too. Every eligible young man was drafted."

"Were you ever drafted, Dad?"

"Molly." Mom waves her to be quiet.

"There's nothing secret about it, Susan. I just never thought the girls would be interested." Lisa and I look at each other. Of course we're interested.

"Thankfully, no. But I did burn my draft card."

"Really?" I can't believe my dad was a draft dodger. "But couldn't you have gotten thrown in jail for that?"

"Yes, but I wouldn't serve in a war I thought was wrong. As it turned out, I graduated from college in 1972, and soon after, Nixon started withdrawing troops from Vietnam, so luckily my draft number never came up. But over fifty thousand guys died unlucky."

"But, Dad, wouldn't you have felt differently about World War II, considering what Hitler did to the Jews?" Lisa is really into this. I'm just trying to make sense of it all.

Dad shakes his head. "I still wouldn't have wanted to kill people. There's no question Hitler and the Japanese needed to be stopped. But did we need to bomb Hiroshima? It's hard to know."

"So did you march in peace rallies and stuff like that?"

"Yes, he did, Carrie. That's where I met him."

"You were a hippie, too, Mom?" Lisa, Molly, and I all start laughing. Gram had shown us pictures of Dad with long hair and bell-bottoms, but we'd never seen any of Mom.

Dad pinches Mom's arm and she blushes. "Well, not really. Our sorority helped clean up after a march, and in came your father with some trash."

"I think we've talked about this enough for one night." Dad gets up and starts clearing the table.

"I supported your father, though it was hard," Gram says in a quiet voice. "The country wasn't ready in 1970 to deal with war resisters and the possible immorality of that war. Neither was your grandfather. He had served America bravely during World War II and believed you fought when your country asked you to, no matter what."

The table is quiet again until Mom gets up and asks who wants chocolate ice cream for dessert. Just then the doorbell rings.

"Oh, no, that's Jeff and I'm not even ready yet. Carrie, go get it and tell him I'll be right there. And talk to him, will you? That is, if you know how."

"Gee, Lisa. I'm sorry, but I flunked Small Talk 101. Maybe Molly better do it."

But Mom taps my arm and motions me out the door. I get up, groaning.

I study myself in the hall mirror as I walk by and think, This is one boy who is not going to wish he were dating the sister instead. Opening the door, I force a smile.

"Oh, it's you."

"Well, who did you think it was going to be, Princess Di?"

"No, Lisa's date, Jeff. Come on in. We're just starting dessert."

When we reach the dining room, Mad goes right over to Gram and gives her a hug.

"Hello, Madeline," Mom says, almost choking on her ice cream.

"Hi, I just came over to see how the sicko was doing."

"So I'm the sicko now," Gram says, smiling.

"Hey, Carrie Ann, have you asked Gram about the quints yet?"

"What quints? What are you talking about?" Molly says, jumping up and pulling on my sleeve. "Mom, make Carrie tell me. She's been teasing me all day."

"Molly, dear," Gram says, patting her hand. "I think it has something to do with the dolls."

"That's right. Carrie's been hogging the dolls, too."

"Hold your horses. I'll go get them."

Mad follows me, and we race to my new room. She comes in behind me, panting. "We sure have Molly going, don't we?"

I take the box from under the bed. Mad starts checking things out again, but I grab her arm. "Come on. Let's go."

Out in the hall, I can't help stopping outside my old room. If only Mad weren't with me right now, I could take one quick look in that box on the bed.

"What's wrong, Carrie?"

"Nothing," I say, heading toward the dining room. I wish I could tell somebody. Somebody who could keep a secret.

Chapter Six

THIS CLINIC is so lifeless and cold. I don't know why I begged Dad to let me come with Gram for her chemo treatment this morning. Gram hasn't said a word since Dad dropped us off a half hour ago.

Like Sunday after church—she made Dad drive us all over to mass at St. Augustine's so she could see her friends. And then afterward she didn't even want to talk to them. Said her back hurt and that she wanted to go home.

Now she just sits here in the waiting room, tapping her fingers on her purse. How does she expect me to read when she's fidgeting like that? Her nails are so long and beautiful. She never used to wear nail polish, but now she has her nails done every week. Says her new long and strong nails are the only good thing about chemo.

Gram looks off today, somehow. Maybe she didn't get her wig on straight. For a while she just kept cutting her hair shorter. But then her hair started coming out, until she was practically bald. One time I was brushing her hair and huge clumps started falling out. After that, she got a wig. Mom, Lisa, and I went to help her buy one at this special wig shop that helps cancer patients.

Gram's going to look worse tomorrow. I'll never forget the time I saw her in January after her first chemo treatment. Her face had no color except for the dark circles under her eyes. And she couldn't eat, always feeling nauseous, like she was going to throw up, but usually she didn't. She just drank herbal tea to settle her stomach.

I can't believe she's had to go through this for six months. It better help her, that's all I can say. But is it? One good week a month. That's what Gram told me last night. Two weeks to get over it and then one week right before the treatment starts wearing off. It's not fair.

Finally we're called in. A lab techie type leads Gram into a cubicle so she can draw some blood. She tries to make small talk, and that forces both Gram and me to smile at her even though we wish she'd be quiet. Gram has bruises up and down her arm, especially around the elbow joint. I let out a gasp, but Gram pats my hand and says, "It's nothing to worry about. It's just from taking blood."

After that, we take the elevator up to Dr. Gonzales's offices. I check in at the front desk and then we wait some more. Finally, a nurse wearing huge, bright pink-and-green earrings and matching necklace comes out to get us. How does she get away with all that ugly jewelry?

Gram introduces me to Lulu. Lulu. What kind of name is that for a fifty-year-old woman? Oh, who am I to talk? How is Carrie Ann going to sound when I'm an old lady?

It seems as though she and Gram are great buddies. I guess that makes sense, since Gram comes here a lot. Lulu has a pretty good figure for an older woman, and she hasn't had her breasts removed, if you know what I mean.

First, Lulu weighs Gram, all the while chatting about the beautiful weather and how grand it was that it didn't rain yesterday so she could plant her garden.

"You're staying steady, Ann. Keep it up." Lulu writes something on the chart and then escorts us into a small examining room. She helps Gram sit down and then asks, "So how have you been feeling this week, Ann? Are you taking your vitamins?"

"Yes, but I'm a little more tired than usual. I moved out of my big house this week, and it took its toll."

Lulu pats Gram's hand. "I know. But now you have this darling granddaughter to keep you company." Lulu then looks at me. "Are you all right, dear? You look a little pale."

"Oh, don't worry about Carrie Ann. She's just got that fair Irish skin, you know." I fake a smile at Lulu and brace for the comment on my hair. But Lulu just visits with Gram for a while and then leaves, saying Dr. Gonzales will be in shortly.

I like Dr. Gonzales. She's young and very businesslike, with her hair pulled back in a low ponytail and no-nonsense talk, but she gives you the feeling of caring, too.

And she's real patient with Gram. They talk for a few minutes, and then Dr. Gonzales suggests that I get some juice down in the cafeteria for Gram to drink during the treatment. I think she just wants to get rid of me, but that's okay. I feel like getting out of there.

I go outside for a breath of fresh air and then buy the juice. When I get back upstairs, Gram is already reclining in this big La-Z-Boy chair in a small room down the hall. And Lulu is rolling this IV cart with a big bottle on it into the room. She pushes it right over to Gram's chair and then, without even waiting, just sticks this huge needle into Gram's hand. It looks like it would hurt, but Gram doesn't even wince.

Last night Gram told me it takes about two hours for the pink fluid, the adriamycin, to drip into her veins. She said there would be a VCR in the room if I wanted to bring a movie, but we decided not to. Now I wish we had. I was hoping Gram would talk some more about when she was a kid, but instead she suggests we say some Hail Marys. Gram has always told me that if you pray for something on Monday, your wish will come true by the end of the week.

Her wish is always that God will help her handle this illness the best she can. That's why she always wants her appointments on Monday or Tuesday, so that the prayers will get her through the week.

After we say a decade of the rosary, we say a prayer to St. Anne. "Remember, Carrie, Saint Anne is the patron saint of women and children. So we can both take a nap, knowing she is protecting us." And with that, Gram closes her eyes.

I put two chairs together and stretch out my legs. I think about writing Sally a letter, but instead pull out Lisa's latest issue of *Seventeen*. She left it for me on the kitchen table this morning. Flipping through it, I start reading the article on how to be a better listener.

But I can't concentrate. Maybe it's the harsh lighting. How can Gram sleep? I get up and turn off the light, and instantly the room is plunged in darkness. All that can be heard is the slight gurgling of the tall, gangly machine that's supposedly carrying the cure for Gram's cancer. Will it work? Or will it just kill all the healthy cells that give Gram her energy?

A while later, I wake up, my neck all stiff. Looking around, I wonder how long I've been asleep. My magazine has fallen on the floor. But Gram is awake and smiling at me. "Gram, I'm sorry. How long have you been awake?"

"Oh, I never really sleep here. Turn on the light, dear, and let me get a look at you. You are so beautiful. You know, your father thinks you look a lot like me." I smile. I'd like to look like Gram. "And you're growing up so fast."

I turn on the light and start to shiver. I wonder how much time is left. No, I came for Gram. It must be hard going through this alone. Mom or Dad have come a few times. But sometimes I think people do things like this out of duty. I don't ever want people doing things for me out of obligation.

"How are you doing, Gram? Does it hurt?"

"Not now. It's the nausea afterward that's the hard part."

"Gram, I'm glad you're living with us now." Gram nods but doesn't smile.

"Have you opened the Billy box yet?" Now why did I say that? I promised myself I wouldn't ask again, at least for a while and especially not today. What a big mouth I have. "I'm sorry, Gram. I shouldn't have said that."

She holds up the hand that doesn't contain the needle. "Carrie, it was so long ago. I don't know if I will."

"But, Gram, aren't you curious about what's in there?"

"I know what's in the box, honey. I'm just not sure I want to dig up all the memories again. People have the right to keep some things to themselves, you know."

"Like contact lenses."

"Like contact lenses," Gram says, smiling. "I wouldn't worry, though. I don't think Lisa noticed a thing. She's been wearing them for two days now and hasn't complained yet."

"Saved by Gram again." I walk over to the chair, and she strokes my hair with her free hand.

"Thank you so much, Carrie, dear, for coming with me today. You have no idea how much it means to me." Just then Lulu comes barging in and, taking the needle out of Gram's hand, announces that the treatment's over.

She puts a Band-Aid on Gram's needle hand and says, "Just rest a few minutes more, Ann, and then you can go." She leans over and gives Gram a big hug. "God bless you until next time." Then she squeezes my arm. "Nice to meet you, honey. Take good care of this wonderful lady."

"I will." I go out to the reception area and call Dad. When I come back, Gram is trying to sit up. She has to lean on me hard to get out of the chair. It's like her bones just aren't working very well anymore.

Gram seems so much older in the last few weeks. Is that how old age comes? In a rush?

It takes us a little while to get downstairs because we have to take mini-breaks along the way. First we walk across the room, then out to the hall, through the lobby, down in the elevator, and finally out the front door.

On the way home Dad's in a good mood, talking about all these new roofing contracts at work. Gram looks out the window. When we get home, she says she wants to rest.

After being cooped up in that clinic all morning, I just want to get outside. I phone Mad, and we decide to ride to the library to research the quints. Wish there was a book I could look up Billy in or, better yet, a cure for cancer.

The minute we start biking, I regret my decision. Mad may look tough. But she rides like she's in slow motion, pushing those pedals around in molasses with her huge legs. Or maybe I'm just in better shape than I thought.

I shouldn't have quit softball. By the end of summer, I'll probably be a major couch potato. Right now I'm kind of in the middle, on the down side of chubby.

Eventually I get so far ahead that I have to stop in the Safeway parking lot to wait for Mad. She finally bikes up singing, "On the gooood ship *Lollipop*. It's a happy, candy shop . . . na, na, na, na . . ." I start laughing so hard, I almost fall off my bike.

Just like Saturday night when Mad got up on her mincey little toes and started dancing around during the Shirley Temple movie that Gram insisted we rent at the video store. Lisa, Molly, and I joined her while Gram sat on the couch and clapped her hands. By the end, we were all laughing so hard we just collapsed on the floor.

Now, when I finally stop laughing, I look at Mad. "How come when you grow up everything changes?"

"What do you mean?"

"Well, I once saw a picture of Shirley Temple grown up, and she looked terrible, not good looking at all. But in her movies, she's such a darling little girl. Nothing ever turns out the way it starts."

"Well, I was never cute, so I guess I have nothing to lose."

Me, either, I think.

When we get to the library, I park my bike and go in. I'm anxious to find some books about those wars. Mad takes a while, and when she finds me at the computer, she just sticks her nose in my face and says, "So I guess you don't like your bike too much, huh?"

"What are you talking about?"

"You didn't lock it."

"Oh, no. If it's stolen, my parents are going to kill me." Mad stands there grinning while I take off for the door.

Huffing and puffing, she doesn't catch me until I'm outside. "Relax. I locked it up with mine."

"I can see that." I glare at her and start back into the library.

"Well, aren't you even going to thank me?"

"Thanks," I say, marching back over to the computer. But Mad doesn't follow me.

Several seconds later, I can hear her very loud voice at the reference desk. "I need information about the Dionne quints; you know, the ones who were born in Canada a billion years ago."

"Could you please wait your turn?" the librarian says.

I run over and grab her arm. "Come here. I'll show you."

I type *Dionne* into the computer, and a couple of titles about the quints come up on the screen. "There you go. Write down the titles and call numbers and go find them."

After a minute, she asks in a quiet voice, "Aren't you coming?"

"No, I want to check on some other books."

"Well, let's do it together."

"Since when are you into togetherness?" Mad has this little-lost-girl look on her face, something I've never seen before.

"I don't know how to do it."

"Oh, come off it. You're not that stupid."

"You know how much I hate school," she yells, standing there with her hands on her hips.

"Excuse me. Could you girls please do your talking somewhere else?" Mad's favorite librarian again.

I drag Mad into the stacks. "You are going to get us kicked out of here."

"You're the one who doesn't believe me."

"Come on," I say, grabbing her arm. I start walking until I find the CT998 section. "Here they are. Check them out, while I go look for my books."

After a while, Mad finds me. "Look. Three whole books on the Dionnes." She opens one and starts reading out loud, her voice getting higher and higher. I glance up, and the librarian is looking over at us. "Come on. Let's get out of here."

When we get in the check-out line, Mad says, "I don't have a card."

"Why am I not surprised?"

"Shut up, would you? I am sick of your superior attitude. I had one, but then I lost it and my mom won't get me another one."

"So get one yourself."

"You have to have a parent signature."

"That never stopped you before."

People in front of us are eavesdropping, so I turn the other way—just in time to see Becky and Nancy at the reference desk. Hopefully, they haven't seen me.

"Okay. Give me your books and I'll check them out on my card. You can unlock the bikes."

"Hey, look over there. Isn't that the girl you skipped school with *and* the guy on our bus that you had the hots for?"

I sneak a look. Nancy and Becky are standing around talking to Joe Kowalski and Leon Johnson. In fact, Nancy is hanging all over Joe. What a flirt. Sometimes I think she used to hang out with me just because Joe rode my bus. No worry that they'll look this way now. Nancy's got her hands full.

When we get home, Mad asks if she can come in to see

Gram. But Gram's curtains are closed, and Mom's car is in the driveway.

"I don't think this is a good time. I'll call you tonight if Gram's up for visitors."

"You'd better." As I start to open the garage, wondering why Mom is home so early, Mad calls out, "Jealous of Nancy flirting at the library?"

I shrug my shoulders.

"Me, too."

"Really? You have a funny way of showing it."

"That's the secret, Carrie. Never let your feelings show."

Molly's standing in the kitchen, pacing the floor, when I walk in. "Where have you been? Something really bad has happened to Gram."

I throw my backpack on the chair and run over to her. "What are you talking about?"

Molly shakes her head and starts crying. "What happened to Gram?" When Molly still doesn't answer, I head for Gram's room.

"Don't. Mom's in there with her. We're supposed to watch for the ambulance."

"Ambulance?"

I start shaking Molly. Sometimes that's the only way to get her to focus. "What is going on?" I feel like I'm screaming.

Molly finally stops crying, but shallow gasps of air keep coming out. "When I got home from swim practice . . . and you weren't around . . ."

"Yeah . . ."

"Well, I went to Gram's room to check on her. But she wasn't there. Then I heard this moaning coming from the bathroom. But I was too scared to go in there alone. Where were you?"

"At the library. Tell me what happened."

"I knew I couldn't just leave Gram like that. So I finally forced myself to go in. There she was, collapsed on the floor. . . . I tried to help her up, but she kept moaning something about her hip.

"Carrie, she looked so awful. Her face and lips were gray, and she was hardly breathing. I just stood there looking at her, not knowing what to do. I hated to leave her, and my legs were shaking so hard, but I knew I had to do something. I called Dad, but he was out on some roofing job. And Mom wasn't at her desk, and Lisa was busy with a customer. I called you at Mad's, but nobody answered. And Gram just kept moaning. Finally I called Mr. Kingston, but he wasn't home either."

"Molly, is Gram all right?" I'm so scared right now, I'm surprised the words come out.

"Well, I was about to call 911 when Mom called back and said she would be right home. She told me to call Gram's doctor. The doctor said Gram's probably broken something because her bones are so brittle. So the ambulance is coming to take Gram to Holy Family Hospital, where Dr. Gonzales will be waiting."

"But is she going to be all right?" I feel the tears pool up in my eyes.

"I don't know. I don't know," Molly keeps saying, just as the ambulance pulls up outside. I open the front door and take the medics to Gram's room. As they load Gram onto the stretcher, I tell Mom I'm going to the hospital.

"No, you and Molly stay here and wait to hear from Dad and Lisa."

"Please, Mom." I grab her arm, my nails digging into her skin.

"No! She just broke something. That's all." But I know it's worse than that. Gram is lying motionless on the stretcher, her cheeks quivering in pain, as they carry her through the living room.

Holding her hand, I walk down the sidewalk with her,

even though Mom shakes her head at me. "Good-bye, Gram. I'll see you soon. We'll be praying for you, Gram." Mom gets into the back of the ambulance and mouths the words "thank you" to me.

As they slam the back of the ambulance doors, I feel the tears come down my cheeks. It's just a broken bone. That's what the doctor said. So why does it feel like so much more?

Chapter Seven

THE PHONE RANG soon after the ambulance takes off. It's Dad. He's so difficult to talk to over the phone that it's hard to explain everything to him. Finally he says he'll just go directly to Holy Family and call us when he knows something.

Molly is still crying when I hang up. "You have no idea how scary it was to find Gram like that. Why weren't you here?"

I try to talk to her, reassuring her that she did the right thing. But then the phone rings again. Lisa—practically hysterical on the other end. Says she's coming right home to drive us to the hospital. Where is all this emotion coming from? I just feel numb inside.

By the time Lisa gets home, Dad has already called to say that we are definitely not to come. Gram has broken her hip, and they have to set it. She's in a great deal of pain and can't handle visitors.

But we're family, I want to scream over the phone. Dad must have sensed my feelings. "You can visit her tomorrow. I promise."

Lisa cancels her date with Jeff, and I put some chicken pot pies in the oven for dinner. Now we're just sitting at the table, waiting for something to happen.

"Let's play with Gram's dolls," Molly says. Lisa starts laughing, but I run into our bedroom and get them. Then Molly helps me arrange the quints on the table.

"These are so cool," Molly says. "So tiny, kinda like the dolls I used to play with."

"Except," I say, "these have real names. See? Emilie, Cecile, Annette, Marie, and Yvonne. Right here on their high chairs and strollers."

"Look at their darling clothes," Lisa says, picking up a little pink dress.

"I got a book about them at the library today."

"When you should have been home with me," Molly says.

"What does the book say?" Lisa asks.

I open it up and start reading: "Born in Canada in 1934 but became famous all over the world. Everybody sent them presents and money because their family was really poor. Girls everywhere had quint dolls of different sizes." Madeline was right.

Lisa holds one in her hand. "When did Gram get these?"

"Gram's mother gave them to her on her ninth birthday."

"Oh, Carrie, you're such a know-it-all where Gram's concerned."

"Molly, lay off, especially tonight," Lisa says as she gets up to clear the table.

"But Carrie, did Gram say we could play with the dolls? Aren't they antiques? I heard Dad say there's real money in doll collecting."

"Well, I heard Gram say that they are for us and our children," Lisa says dramatically. Molly and I start laughing.

Lisa picks up one of my books on Vietnam and starts flipping through the pages. "Isn't it wild that Mom and Dad met at a peace march?" she says, showing us a picture of some hippies carrying a big HELL NO, WE WON'T GO banner.

Molly curls up her nose as she points to a guy with long,

mangy hair and a scruffy beard. "Do you think Dad really looked like this?"

"Let's find out," I say, getting up and looking around. "Where are those old picture albums?" We're about to head to the basement when Mom and Dad walk in.

"Girls, sit down." Dad has that head-of-the-household look on his face. "Why wasn't somebody home with Gram?"

Molly and I look at each other across the kitchen table. "You never told us somebody had to be here all the time. I went to chemo with her, and then she wanted to rest. So I decided to go to the library."

"Well, you shouldn't have left until Molly got home."

"But, Dad, Molly's hardly *ever* home. And you never said that somebody had to be here all the time." My throat starts to choke up. How could he think that I would ever do anything to hurt Gram?

"Will, Will. Your mother just moved in. We haven't even had time to figure out schedules yet."

"I didn't know we needed to. I thought they'd care enough to be here with their grandmother."

"I do, I do." I feel the tears start coming down my cheeks again. Why am I crying so much? Why does Dad always jump to conclusions? "How is she? Aren't you even going to tell us how Gram is?"

Dad and Mom give each other a look. Then Mom says, "The pin's all set, and she's finally sleeping peacefully."

"What time can I go see her tomorrow?"

"Yeah," Molly and Lisa join in.

"Not tomorrow, girls. Gram's having tests all day. They're doing a bone scan to find out how brittle her other bones are."

"But, Dad, you promised, and I know she'd want some company—"

"Carrie. We'll talk about it tomorrow night after her tests are completed."

* * *

Dad looks terrible at dinner tonight. He has circles under his eyes, like he hasn't slept in a week. He didn't go to work today. Spent the day with Gram at the hospital.

It's worse than a broken hip. I know it. All day this lump has been growing in my stomach, growing and growing, and now it's moving up to my mouth. I can't eat. Later it'll probably reach my brain, and I won't be able to think.

"Girls." Dad reaches for Mom's hand, then starts again. "Girls, Gram has cancer all through her bones. That's why her hip broke. Now the doctors say it's spreading to her brain."

"Her brain?" Lisa squeaks out. "Isn't that—?"

"Fatal. Yes. She may not have very long to live." I look down at my plate, trying to process his words. "A few weeks, six months, maybe even a year. They just don't know. But don't forget Gram's tough."

"How could it spread so fast? I don't understand. People have cancer for years, and a lot of them get better." My voice is shaking. Mom hands me a Kleenex.

"Because, unfortunately, honey, not all cancers are alike. Will, we'd better make a clean slate of this."

My dad nods. "Your grandmother has had cancer for years. She first got breast cancer when Carrie was a baby, before Molly was even born."

I pound my hand on the table. "Why do there always have to be secrets in this family?"

Dad comes over and puts his hands on my shoulders. "Carrie, you were a baby. Lisa a toddler. We told you when her cancer recurred in January."

"Is that why Gram sold her house and moved in with us?" I've never heard Lisa's voice so serious.

Dad nods, then takes a deep breath and continues. "Gram found out the cancer had spread to her bones in April, when she sprained her ankle in Washington, D.C. Now the brain. I had no idea it would spread so quickly."

"But why couldn't you have told us then?" Lisa sounds angry, just like I feel.

"Because Gram didn't want people to know. She wanted to keep up her regular schedule as long as possible," Mom says.

"But we're her family. We should know," Lisa says, getting up from the table.

"Carrie knew. She kept telling us something was wrong." Molly is crying now, too. "But Lisa and I just ignored her." Molly starts jiggling the table with her leg.

"Molly, stop moving the table," I yell out.

"So what now, Dad?" Lisa asks.

"The doctors say that as the cancer spreads in her brain, she'll start acting more confused, losing her memory. And all her bones are very brittle. She could break another one at any time."

"So we'll all have to help take care of Gram when she comes home next week." Mom looks around at us.

"Home? Home to die?"

"Yes, Molly. Nowadays cancer patients often spend their last days at home."

I stand up and pound the table again. "Stop talking about dying. You act like Gram's just going to give up. She's a fighter. She's going to get better—she has to."

Later, I lie in bed, hitting my head on the pillow. Why does everybody I care about have to be taken away? I said that Gram would fight this. But can she?

"Carrie, are you awake?"

"Yeah."

"You're right. Gram can get better. Mom and Dad are acting like it's a sure thing. But my coach always says nothing's for sure until you touch the wall. And they're coming up with new cures every day. And like you said, Gram's a fighter."

"But how do you fight brain cancer, Molly?"

"I don't know. But there has to be a way."

I don't say anything, and pretty soon I hear Molly's steady breathing.

I try to sleep, but I can't. One week Gram is living in her own house, taking care of her garden, and the next week she's lying alone in a hospital room, dying of brain cancer. Could there be a miracle cure like Molly says?

All the things I still haven't done with her. All the things I don't know about her. I'm just beginning to learn about Gram's life as a girl. She's such a good person. Why does she have to die?

My stomach starts to growl, so I get up and head for the kitchen. Walking down the hall, I hesitate outside Gram's room, then go in. Just to be near her, to feel the warmth of her quilt, to twirl her small black rosary beads in my fingers.

The moonlight is streaming through the window, right onto the Billy box sitting on the floor next to Gram's favorite chair. I stoop down and touch it, tracing the name "Billy" with my finger. What if Gram dies and I never find out what's in this box?

She's in so much pain now, she probably doesn't even care about it. I was sure that after the chemo, when she felt better, she would invite me into her room to show me the contents.

But now all that's changed. I punch the box. I hate cancer. I hate secrets. Why can't people just be honest? Well, I'm going to find out the truth, at least about this.

As I open the box, the lid feels fragile in my fingers. So old. Should I be doing this? On the very top of the box are two packets of letters written on thin, blue stationery and wrapped in ribbons. So it *is* letters. I was right.

The first bundle is addressed to Ann Sweeney, 270 Liberty Street, San Francisco, California. The second, to PFC William Sweeney, #2358635, APO 7, San Francisco, California.

William Sweeney. He must be Billy.

I look through the box. At the bottom is an old green khaki army hat with "William Sweeney" printed in the inside rim and the ID number 2358635. Then I pull out a rectangular metal piece on a chain engraved with the same number as in the address—2358635. It must be his dog tag number. I remember an old war movie on TV where the soldiers all had to use their dog tags or serial number for everything. The army cared more about the ID number than your name.

Mom was watching it with me and explained it was like our social security numbers of today. I hate it when I'm treated like a number. I'm Carrie Ann O'Leary. That's what I want to be known as, no matter how many times I've threatened to change my name.

William Sweeney. Billy Sweeney. Who is he? Sweeney. That's right. Gram's maiden name was Sweeney. So is he a relative of Gram's?

I look through the box again and pull out three small navy blue cases. The first one contains a gold Good Conduct medal attached to a ribbon with red-and-white stripes. The second box has a bronze medal inscribed with the words AMERICAN CAMPAIGN—WORLD WAR II. It has a ship and plane on the front and a ribbon with red, white, blue, and black stripes.

The third box is the most special. It contains the Purple Heart. I've heard of that. It's actually a gold heart with a glass inlay of purple and a ribbon with purple-and-white stripes. On the back is inscribed WILLIAM SWEENEY, FOR MILITARY MERIT. So he fought in World War II. If he got the Purple Heart, does that mean he died?

I don't get it. He's a war hero. If he's related to Gram, why hasn't she ever talked about him? And why doesn't Dad know about him?

I unfasten the first packet of letters and begin reading.

December 14, 1941

Dearest Billy,

I miss you so much. It wasn't so bad when you were in the National Guard and went to training just on weekends. But now that you're in the regular army and especially since last Sunday, I feel even worse about it.

You kept saying that war was coming. But how did you know, Billy? How did you know the Japanese were planning that sneak attack on Pearl Harbor?

How I wish you'd been here—a horrible twist to a lovely Sunday afternoon. I was baby-sitting the O'Brien girls and we were listening to *The Jack Benny Show* on the radio. But then they interrupted the show with this special news bulletin about Pearl Harbor. Kathleen and Grace got really scared and started crying. And then Mother called right away to say that Dad was coming over to get us.

Later I took out my old paper dolls to distract the girls. It did seem to stop their tears until their parents came to get them. But now *I* feel like crying all the time because in one short week, dear brother, everything has changed.

I feel like I'm not a girl anymore, that I should get rid of everything frivolous in my life. So I cleaned out my closet and decided to give away all my dolls to the O'Brien girls. But Mother threw a fit and said she'd spent too much money on the dolls for me to just throw them out. Sometimes I think those dolls are more for her than me.

She said I should save them for my daughters.

Daughters? I'm only in high school and we're in the middle of a war. How can I think about getting married and having children? Mother's getting on my nerves, but Rose said just to let her be. It's easy for her. She's busy with her office job and gets to work at the USO at night.

Oh, Billy, how I'm going on so. How are you? How is your training going in San Luis Obispo? I was walking along the beach last Saturday before all this happened. I looked out at the ocean and pretended that you too were watching the waves and thinking of us.

I wish you could get leave so you could be with us for Christmas. But I'd better stop dreaming. When you finally do get to visit, I promise not to cry so hard when you leave.

Love,
Ann

Paper dolls, San Francisco. Ann has to be Gram. So Billy is her brother? That would make him my great-uncle Billy. No lover out of the past. Just a brother. What's to keep secret about that?

Chapter Eight

I WAKE UP THIS MORNING tired and confused. But then I remember the letters. I had stayed awake past midnight reading them, but now they're all blending together in my mind. Molly's long gone to swim practice, so it's safe to get them out.

December 21, 1941

Dear Annie,

Just got your letter and it looks like I won't be home for Christmas. Funny you should mention the ocean. I look out at it all the time and think of you, too. Some of the hospital work is pretty menial but most of the time it's interesting. So much to learn about the human body. And I'd much rather be doing this than marching up and down the beach. I do have to participate in some drills, but at least I'm not carrying a gun.

Sis, there are no books down here. Could you send me some? Most of the guys don't like to read. They'd rather just listen to the radio or play poker. So for those few of us readers there is nothing. I should have gone to college like Dad wanted. But I was sick of studying and National Guard duty didn't pay enough for college tuition.

444 jumping jacks and 85 push-ups every day. You wouldn't recognize me with my tough body and the stubble on my head.

December 27, 1941

Dearest Billy,

It was such a lonely Christmas without you. I *loved* the gold necklace you sent me. And your picture. You are so handsome! I'm not the only one who thinks so, believe me. I put that silly school picture of me on the other side of the locket and now wear it around my neck every day.

Billy, it just wasn't the same without you at midnight mass this year and we missed your voice around the piano, singing carols. You always covered up my mistakes on the piano. Mother must have said at least five times that this was the first time the family had been apart at Christmas.

We have blackouts at night now. You must, too. Last night some man from the civil defense agency came by and asked if Dad would be our block warden. Now he goes around every night to make sure all the lights in our neighborhood are off.

Everybody's so afraid the Japanese might bomb us next. Yesterday downtown they were putting huge sandbags around all the big buildings in case they do.

In spite of your not being here for the holidays, Mother and Dad are holding up remarkably well. For being a quiet man, I'm surprised about how excited Dad is to be block warden. I guess after years of being out of work, this makes him feel useful.

The house is so empty without you. At night during the blackouts, it's especially hard. I wish I could just knock on your door and you'd be there to tell me jokes in the dark.

They aren't allowing any civilian travel on the trains right now so it was hard on people wanting to get home for Christmas. The trains are all jammed with soldiers. Do you have any idea where you'll be sent? Wherever you end up, I'll be proud you are serving our country. But I secretly hope you can stay in California and just help the wounded soldiers coming home.

February 14, 1942

Annie—

What a way to spend Valentine's Day, stuck on a ship going who knows where. Then again, yesterday I couldn't have written at all, I was so seasick. These huge waves just rocking the boat, rocking the boat. I wish I could say that the scenery was beautiful, but all you can see is miles and miles of ocean on every side. I don't even know what direction we're headed.

It's strange not to be in California. Some of the guys are excited to finally be headed for some war action. I just help sick and wounded soldiers so it doesn't really matter where I am. At least that's what I keep telling myself.

Yesterday, though, I wanted to leap off this ship and swim home. They just announced that we're now in a war zone, which means our letters will be censored, and they don't want us to keep a journal. Security risk if the Japanese got ahold of it.

March 20, 1942

Dearest Billy,

I think about you every minute and can't help feeling sad. I should be happy about playing the part of Alice in the school play (I have to wear a blonde wig!). Catherine Kelly was so jealous. She thought she had the part all sewed up because she is a natural blonde. I got a B- on my algebra test today!!!!!! You know how I hate math! So I was thrilled. But I don't know how I did it without your tutoring.

Tom Johnson came over from St. Ignatius to walk me home from school today. He wants me to go to the prom with him next month. Some of the girls will be jealous because he's a senior, but he talks too much. I can't get a word in edgewise. I wish he were more like you and knew when to be quiet. Maybe I just wish he would listen more to what I have to say. Is that asking too much?

He went on and on about how lucky you were to be able to defend our country against Hitler. Finally I interrupted and said you were serving on the Pacific Front. And he said that's even better because the Japs are such monsters.

Are they, Billy? They moved all the Japanese families out of the city and into internment camps in the desert. Remember the girl wearing the kimono who waited on us at the Japanese Tea Garden the day before you left? She's probably gone now, too. She was so pretty and nice. It doesn't seem fair. Many of them have never even been to Japan.

Oh, how I'm going on so. I miss you so much.

Love,
Annie

P.S. This is me in front of the Christmas tree. My hair's too short and my lips look funny, but then I never claimed to be the gorgeous one in the family. That's your role.

I study the picture and try to imagine Gram as a girl of sixteen with an older brother she's crazy about. She is cute, with her dark hair and mischievous smile.

I put the black-and-white photo down. Now, over fifty years later, she's not cute anymore. She might be dying. Brain cancer. Terminal, that's what the doctor said.

All the things I still don't know about her. And Billy. I just can't believe she never told us about her brother Billy. But at least I have these letters, a part of her life that's long gone. I'm going to read these letters over and over and take notes on things I don't understand. Then later, when I'm brave, I can ask Gram about them.

I hear a noise down the hall. Who could it be? Everybody else left hours ago.

"Carrie, are you home? Carrie?"

I run out into the hall to find Mad walking toward me. She looks angry.

"Why didn't you answer the door, for Pete's sake?"

"Well, why didn't you knock? Do you always just barge into people's houses?"

I can't let her into my room. The letters are all over the bed. So I manage to convince her to wait in the kitchen until I'm dressed. Over breakfast I tell her about Gram's broken hip and brain cancer and everything. I start to cry again.

"It's okay, Carrie. Everything's going to be okay."

"No, it's not. Gram's going to die."

"I know. I know." I hear a catch in Mad's voice. When I look up, there are tears in her eyes. She comes over and hugs me, and I don't even feel embarrassed.

When she breaks away, she tells me she's going to swamp me in gin rummy. We play, but I can't concentrate. I keep thinking about those letters.

Finally, Mad throws down her cards. "This is too easy. Let's do something else."

"Maybe you'd better go. I have to clean my room."

"No, you don't. How messy could it be? You know you're just going to mope around."

"Well, wouldn't you if your grandmother was dying of cancer?"

"Probably. But I only have one grandparent that I know of, and he's drunk half the time. I know what *he's* going to die of, and it's not cancer."

"I'm sorry."

Mad gets up and starts opening our cupboards. "Don't be. I just don't come from the all-American family like you do."

"I think your mom's great."

"You do?"

"Yeah. She's fun. Not all rigid and businessy like my mother." Mad starts opening drawers. "What are you doing?"

She gives me a look, but comes back and sits down. "Your mother is gorgeous."

"Gorgeous mother, gorgeous sisters. That's my problem."

"So? You look like your dad."

"I know. Another one of my problems."

"Honey, you don't know the meaning of problems," Mad says, picking up the salt and pepper shakers. She sure is hyperactive. Just like Molly. So why isn't she skinny like Molly?

"I do now. Gram's dying."

"You don't know that for sure."

"Well, my parents certainly think so."

"And you believe everything your mother says, like a good little girl."

I lean over and punch her, right through her soft stomach. All she does is laugh and then puts the shakers down.

"Let's go over to my house."

"Your house?" Mad never wants to be at her house. It's like she's always trying to escape it.

"Yeah. Let's go." Mad heads for the door.

"No, I'd better stay here in case the hospital calls or something."

"Put the answering machine on." I shake my head, thinking about the letters again. "Come on. You always ask about my room. Now's your chance to see it."

All of a sudden I feel funny. What if there are marijuana plants growing in the backyard or something? Mad's mom is still kind of a hippie. Maybe that's why Mad never wants to be home.

"But what if Gram gets worse? Dad was really upset when I wasn't here the day Gram broke her hip."

"So are you chained to the house all summer?"

"Well, I was supposed to be grounded for two weeks because of my grades, but now that Gram's so sick, my parents seem to have forgotten it."

"If I was grounded over the years for my grades, I'd never see the light of day. Come on." She grabs my arm. "Just for half an hour. She can't die in half an hour."

"You're sick."

"No, your gram is. Oh, god, I can't believe I just said that. I'm sorry. I'm really sorry. I really like your gram. I'm sorry."

"It's okay. Will you stop saying you're sorry and will you please stop jumping around? You're making me nervous. I'll come, but just for thirty minutes. First I have to record a message."

I press the button, and when the red light flashes on, I start speaking. "Hi, this is the O'Learys. We can't come to the phone right now, but please leave a message. If this is the hospital and my grandmother is worse, please call Carrie at 456-6765."

"That's a pretty strange message."

"You're right. I'm not coming." I start to turn the machine off.

Mad stops me. "It's fine. Let's go."

On the way over to her house, Mad brings up Lisa, of all people. "Does she have a lot of dates?"

"Why would you care?"

"I don't know. You just said Lisa canceled a date the other night, and I was curious. She goes out all the time, doesn't she? I've seen the guys driving up. Does she like them?"

"Who knows? She's always seems to be rolling her eyes behind their backs."

"I wonder what it's like to have lots of guys with the hots for you."

"You act so tough, but you talk just like other girls. Guys, guys, guys."

"Oh, so you thought fat girls don't like boys?"

What could I say to that? I just know that boys don't usually go for fat girls. But they don't go for me, either. Is that because I'm half fat?

I'll bet it's been two years since I've been inside Mad's house. It's pretty much like ours, ranch style like the whole subdivision. Except her mom has this great Japanese tea garden out front. Everybody in the neighborhood oohs and ahs over it but then gossips about the two of them behind their backs.

When we walk into the kitchen, Mad's mother is sitting, reading the newspaper. Last night's dishes are piled in the sink, and Mad's bowl of half-eaten cereal is still on the table. Her mother is eating a bowl of granola.

She looks up and smiles, not embarrassed at all. My mother has a fit if one thing is out of place when people come over.

"Why, Carrie, it's so nice to see you."

"Hi." I don't know what else to say. I like your beads?

"I'm so sorry your grandmother isn't feeling well. She's such a wonderful woman."

"It's worse than that, Mrs. Connors, I mean Patty. She has bone cancer and broke her hip and now the doctors think the cancer is spreading to her brain."

"Oh, no."

"And she might not last through the summer."

"Oh, Carrie, I'm so sorry." She gets up and puts her arm around me.

"I can't stand to see Gram suffer. She told me once when I broke my arm that she was as wimpy about pain as I am."

"If I know your grandmother, she'll handle it. It's the rest of us I worry about. But you know what they say, Carrie?" I shake my head. "We Irish women can endure pain better than anybody." Does that include me, I wonder?

During all this, Mad has been sitting there eating potato chips.

"Madeline. What about your diet? Why don't you have a piece of fruit instead? And offer Carrie something."

"Mom, stop ragging, okay?"

Madeline's room is neat in more ways than one—rock posters all over the wall and a bookshelf full of tapes and books. I wonder where she gets the money.

"Hey, I thought you didn't know how to read."

"Very funny. My mom's really into books. Gives them to me instead of food."

Mad puts on a Bruce Springsteen tape, and we just sit there, listening to the music. Mad pulls up the shades, and the sun streams through the windows. It feels good to be away from the house—away from Gram's cancer and Billy's letters. I feel free.

Eventually Mad breaks the silence. "All my mom does is bitch at me."

"No, she doesn't."

"How would you know?"

I look at my watch. "I gotta go."

"Come on. Stay a while."

"Thirty minutes, remember?"

"Well, then, I'm coming with you."

When we get back, the red light is blinking on the machine. This is it, I think, pushing the message button. "Carrie, for heaven's sake, why did you leave that message? Your grandmother specifically asked that people not know she's in the hospital. Use better judgment, please. We'll talk about this later."

"And you think *your* mother is a problem?"

"Well, Carrie, it was a stupid message."

"So why didn't you say so before? All I wanted was for the hospital to call me if something happened to Gram," I say, sitting down at the table.

"Right. Like don't you think they'd call your dad at work instead?" Mad straddles a chair backward.

I push her chair, practically knocking her over. But she recovers without falling and then stands up. How can somebody so big be so coordinated?

I point my finger at her and shake my head. "Get out of here."

"I was just leaving."

* * *

It's her loss. I was just about to tell her about the letters. No, I wasn't. She'd probably say, "Once a sneak, always a sneak." It's true. I am a sneak. I don't have a life, so I have to snoop into other people's lives. But somebody had to or we wouldn't know about Uncle Billy or Gram's life during the war or anything.

May 15, 1942

Hi, sis. No letters again today. You'll never know how much your letters mean to me. The weather's so foggy and miserable, I guess it could be even longer until a ship comes in with some mail. Everybody goes nuts around mail time. Then depression sets in when we find out nothing's arrived.

The good news is that some USO entertainers were here a couple of weeks ago—Olivia de Havilland and John Huston. Best time I've had since leaving California. That Olivia sure looks better in person than she did as Melanie in *Gone With the Wind*. Remember when I convinced Mother that you were old enough to see it? And then afterwards you begged me to get you the book?

There's a priest up here who's our chaplain, so I can go to mass whenever I can fit it in. Mother will be happy. In basic training a bunch of us just got together and mumbled prayers. But guys are doing a lot more talking about God now that they realize how close the enemy is.

They finally got the hospital built so we've been busy setting up supplies and furniture. Luckily there haven't been any battles so no wounded to take care of. Just a lot of blisters and colds and hypothermia. A lot of these guys haven't been trained how to dress for the cold.

Keep writing. Take care of Mother and Dad and Rose. I sure miss everybody and your cookies. Hey, how did your debut as Alice go? You never told me.

Love,
Billy

Dad went straight to the hospital tonight to see Gram and talk with the doctors. At dinner Mom tells us that no other visitors are allowed because Gram's in a lot of pain and pretty drugged up on medicine. But she promises that Dad will find out when we can see Gram. Why are they protecting her so much? Wouldn't seeing us make her feel better?

After that depressing news, I can't help asking Mom if Gram had any brothers. "I don't think so. Just her older sister Rose."

It doesn't make sense. If Ann is Gram, why doesn't anybody know about her brother Billy?

"Carrie, about that ridiculous phone message today—"

Mom stops and watches as Lisa sweeps around to the other side of the table and puts her arms around Molly and me. "And I have two sisters. Aren't I lucky?"

Chapter Nine

Another day, and all I want to do is read these letters.

June 9, 1942

Dear Annie,

Man, oh man, oh man. Don't tell Mother and Dad, but last night the Japs bombed us. I was working a late shift at the hospital when out of the sky came these bombers letting loose. It felt like the heavens were opening up.

The power went out. So until they got the emergency generator going, we went around setting up kerosene lamps, and then started moving the patients from the bombed wing. My heart was pounding the whole time. I thought I'd been scared before, but this beats all.

Christmas Eve 1942

I'm pretty lonesome tonight, sis. The hospital crew had a party, enough beer for about two cans around and some sandwiches and soft drinks. The group kept changing since some people had to cover the hospital shift.

One medic played a guitar in the corner and some of us started singing spirituals, of all things. Don't be disappointed, Annie. It just isn't the same, singing Christmas carols without you and the family. Some guys were playing checkers. Nobody talked about the war.

For the past two weeks snow with wind has swept the island. Wild winds that pierce right through you and underneath the snow, black mud that sinks into your clothes. I don't know how the soldiers can stand it day after day. They come into the hospital with frozen toes and cracked lips. But nobody complains.

Next evening

I'm feeling better. Today the three-quarter moon stayed up until we went to eat our Christmas dinner. Served in a Quonset hut with a Christmas tree. Roasted chicken and hot mashed potatoes and peas. Not quite as good as Mom's, but I was happy for once at this mess.

The phone just rang. It was Dad saying I could go visit Gram this afternoon or wait and go with the whole family tonight. He even said he'd give me a ride to the hospital, but I told him I needed the exercise.

The warm sunshine feels good on my shoulders. I keep gulping in fresh air, trying to prepare myself for that awful ammonia hospital smell that tries to wipe away all the smells, good and bad. Like chemo, destroying all the cells.

I go right up to Gram's room, gently pushing her door open and tiptoeing in. She's sleeping. I go over to the side of her bed and study her face. She looks like she's aged ten years in the last three days. Is it the cancer or the broken hip? Or has she given up? No, she can't.

Turning away, I look around. One gurgling machine with a tube attached to Gram's arm. No get-well cards. Why doesn't Gram want her friends to know she's here? White and yellow roses—her favorites. Dad must have brought them.

I pull out a pen and paper from my backpack and start writing.

June 23—2 P.M.

Dear Sally,

How can things change so quickly in one week? Here I thought boredom was going to be my biggest problem this summer, but what I wouldn't give to go back to the way things were. Gram falls and breaks her hip and the next thing we know she's got brain cancer. I feel so empty inside. I can't imagine a life without Gram.

I wish you were here to talk to, that it was like last summer when we biked over to each other's houses whenever we wanted. Now I talk to Fatty Maddie. That's how desperate I am. No, that's not fair. We're actually kind of friends. Molly thinks I'm crazy. Do you?

I stop writing. Is Maddie my friend? I look over at Gram, and her eyes are open. I run over to her bed and hug her.

"Gram, I'm so sorry about all this. I've missed you so much and Dad wouldn't—" Gram slowly puts up her hand.

"I've missed you too, honey."

"I'm so sorry I wasn't home when you broke your hip, Gram."

"Carrie." She takes my hand. Hers feels so weak and cold. "It wasn't your fault."

"But . . ." I feel my throat start to choke up. What's going to happen when she gets worse?

Then suddenly my brain changes tracks, like it's out of control, and I blurt out, "Did you have a brother named Billy?"

Gram's eyes glaze over. Why did I say that?

"Billy? Billy?" I can hardly hear her. "How I loved him. We were as thick as thieves, you know."

"What happened to Uncle Billy, Gram?"

"He died." Then she just closes her eyes, as if to say, "That's enough for today, Carrie."

"How, Gram? When?" I whisper, but I know she's not going to answer me, at least not now.

So she did have a brother Billy. I'm happy in a way that I guessed right, but it's sad and confusing, too. If Gram loved Billy so much, why has she kept him a secret all these years? Was he some awful person or did something terrible happen to him?

I know I should be glad that Gram's sleeping and out of her pain for a while, but there are so many things I want to ask her, and not just about Uncle Billy.

The nurse comes in and says that I might as well go since Gram will probably sleep until dinner. I want to yell out that I'm her granddaughter and that Gram feels safer when I'm here and that's why she fell asleep in the first place. But the nurse just gives me this look. And then I want to scream even louder, Don't you know I love her better than anybody?

But I don't say a word. I leave instead. On the way home I try to tell myself that later I may need the nurse on my side.

When I get home, I collapse on the bed, exhausted. But the letters keep floating across my brain. I can't stay away from them.

May 10, 1943

Dear Sis,

Hard to believe I've been here over a year now and we've never experienced a real battle. There's talk of an invasion soon. They would need medics to go along with the infantry troops. So who knows what's ahead of me. Lots of new soldiers arriving every day.

We had an alert last night. Walked four or five miles in the dark. I just know the commanders are gearing us up for a battle. After all this waiting, maybe it'll be a relief. I've always said I didn't want to carry a gun and nobody's ever given me a bad time about it, at least not too much. But somebody's got to go along to help the wounded soldiers. Don't they?

May 30, 1943

Dearest Annie,

I'm sick at heart. Don't ever let anybody tell you that war is romantic. We lost hundreds of guys at the battle of ██████████. Sure we took the island back and the Japanese lost thousands. But there was blood and bodies everywhere. Who ever decided this was the way to solve world problems?

This is probably going to get censored but I have to write it down. *Don't* show this letter to Mother and Dad, especially Mother. It will just upset her.

I got assigned as the medic for this platoon of forty-seven soldiers. They shipped us into a Japanese-held island and we landed in the middle of the night. Darkness everywhere and we could barely see to set up our tents. The next morning when the sun came up I checked the belt I wore around my waist to make sure it carried all the first aid supplies I needed.

After a quick breakfast, we advanced to the front, looking for the enemy. Some minor gunshot and mortar wounds the first few days, but I didn't lose anybody, even though we saw plenty of dead bodies from other companies. The guys call me Doc. If anything happens to them, I'm the only one they can count on.

One afternoon the platoon sgt. and I were following about fifteen feet back from the front line. Suddenly one of our guys gets hit. When I reach him, he's gushing blood from a gunshot wound in the chest. No matter what I do, I can't get the bleeding to stop.

Jimmy Mitchell, that's his name, keeps going in and out of consciousness. I'd only known him a few days, but I really liked him. He was always telling jokes and trying to get our minds off the war, even though we knew there were Japs around every corner.

Jimmy says, "Doc, I'm not going to make it. Write a letter for me to my son." With all the gunfire around me, I can't hear him, and he has to repeat it. At first I don't want to; I want to keep trying to stop his bleeding. But he insists. So I dig around and find some paper and a pen in my pack and start writing as fast as I can because his voice is fading. My head and hand were numb, but thankfully not my fingers.

When he finished, I wrote down his Seattle address on an envelope and he made me promise to deliver the letter in person to his son and wife in Seattle. Then he asked me to get out the photo in the right side pocket of his pack. By this time, his voice has really faded and I can barely get a heartbeat.

I put the photo of his wife and baby son in both his hands and he said, "Thanks, Doc. You're the best." Then he closed his eyes. I held him in my arms for a while and prayed, even though I knew he was gone.

Poor Uncle Billy. What must it be like to watch someone die? I don't even want to think about it.

I flip through the letters, but there are no more from Billy. My head starts spinning. Did he ever deliver the letter to the

Mitchells? Gram says Billy died, but where? In the war? Where was he stationed? He mentioned cold and snow.

I pull out the World War II book from the library, and look in the index. Not much about the war in the Pacific, mostly Europe. South Pacific, Philippines. It would be warm down there. Alaska. Aleutian Islands. Is that where he died? In the same battle as Jimmy Mitchell? No, he lived to write about the battle.

In the kitchen I can hear Molly banging around. I've got to get out of here and figure out what this all means.

I shove the letters into the box and back under the bed, then sneak out the front door, praying Molly doesn't hear me. If she does, I'll spill the beans, and I don't want the family to know until I figure this out. It's my secret.

I run down the street. I need help. Madeline. She's got street smarts, but what does she know about World War II?

No, Gram. She's the only one who can help me. But she might be so upset I opened the box that she'll get worse.

"Hello, Carrie." I look up.

"Mr. Kingston," I yell, running over to him and throwing my arms around him. "You're back." He's washing his camper, so the hose in his hands sprays all over both of us, but I don't care. Why didn't I think to ask him before?

"Mr. Kingston, you're the only one who can help me right now."

"I'd be happy to be of assistance," he says, calmly walking over to turn off the hose. "Why don't you come inside and I'll get us both towels?"

I nod. "But you have to promise to keep a vow of secrecy."

He holds up his right hand and says, "I do solemnly promise."

Before I know it, we are sitting in his kitchen drying ourselves off while I tell him all about Uncle Billy's letters and how they end before I know where he was or how he died.

"It is hard to know for sure because they did censor all the mail during the war by blackening out place names," he says.

"But do you think my uncle was in Alaska?"

"It sounds like it, from what you say. The Japanese did bomb Dutch Harbor in June 1942 and captured the islands of Attu and Kiska. A year later, in May 1943, American forces won Attu back in one of the bloodiest but least-known battles of the Second World War and the only battle of the war fought on American soil. I should know. I fought in it."

"That's right. You told me that when I interviewed you. Did you know my Uncle Billy Sweeney, Mr. K?"

"I don't think so, Carrie. There were thousands of troops. It *was* an awful three weeks of fighting. We lost almost six hundred men, the Japanese over twenty-five hundred, mostly because they put hand grenades to their heads rather than let us take them prisoner." Mr. Kingston shakes his head and can't talk for a minute.

"Yeah. Uncle Billy wrote that it was pretty bad." Mr. K offers me some lemonade and then starts talking again.

"Our tanks were useless, and the jeeps sank up to their axles in the mud. We had no maps of the islands, so we would just stumble around in the dense fog and darkness and then maybe wake up to find a Jap in the foxhole next to you."

"Uncle Billy wrote about Attu but there are no more letters after that. What do you think happened to him?"

"I don't know about the medics. But most of the infantry troops were later transferred to the South Pacific or Africa."

"What happened next on the islands?"

"Well, some of us stayed on Attu for another six months, making sure the Japanese didn't come back. And three months later, in August 1943, American and Canadian forces invaded the island of Kiska, the last remaining Japanese-held island."

"What happened there?"

"The soldiers landed and then hiked for three days in the

fog before realizing the Japanese had already snuck off the island undetected. Apparently in the confusion the soldiers ended up killing some of their own in friendly fire."

"What do you mean, 'friendly fire'?"

"Accidental shooting by a soldier from your own country."

"How awful."

I want to go home and study the letters to see if they match up to what Mr. K said, but Molly's there. So I sneak my bike out of the garage and go to the library instead.

This time I lock my bike, but I don't have my library card. So I just look at some more World War II books, studying a picture of some soldiers in front of a tent on Attu. Is one of them Uncle Billy, Mr. Kingston, or maybe even Jimmy Mitchell?

I look up to find Joe and Leon standing next to me. I'm surprised Becky and Nancy aren't there, too. Joe and Leon are really friendly, but I can't concentrate on what they're saying. And then I look at my watch. Six P.M. I'm going to get killed.

When I get outside, it's raining. But I bike along, not even caring. I pretend I'm out on the Aleutians with Uncle Billy, maybe caught in a williwaw, that cold, violent wind. A thousand miles out in the Pacific, so close to Japan. It must have been horrible. I could never fight in a war like that. No wonder Gram hates war so much.

When I get home, they're almost finished with dinner. But for once Dad isn't angry.

"Oh, Carrie," Mom says, feeling my jacket. "You're soaking wet." I nod. "Honey, we have to go to the hospital before visiting hours are over. Quick. Go change your clothes. You can eat when we get back."

I turn to Dad. "I visited Gram this afternoon and it was pretty hard. Could I just take a warm shower and see her again tomorrow?"

Dad puts his arm around me. "I understand. I feel the same way sometimes." Molly and Lisa give me these weird looks like they *don't* understand. But they will when they see Gram.

I stand at the window and watch them pull out of the driveway. What happened to Uncle Billy? I have to find out.

After my shower, I go back into the bedroom and take out the Billy box. But as I start to pull out the packets one more time, I see something I've never seen before. Pushed down in one corner is a locket with a delicate gold chain.

My heart is pounding as I open it up. Gram's schoolgirl grin beams at me, and on the other side is a young soldier with an army hat on, handsome and solemn but with a grin like Gram's hidden just below the surface. The locket Uncle Billy gave Gram for Christmas.

My hands are shaking. I'll bet Gram has forgotten about it. I can't wait to show her. What if she's angry I opened the box? No, this will make her want to tell me about Billy.

I take out a clean pair of white socks from my drawer and carefully tuck the locket in one of them and put it under my pillow. Then I feel around the box again, wondering what else might be there that I haven't discovered yet. My fingers touch a lone letter, squished in another corner of the box.

Carefully removing it, I smooth the letter out on the bed. Its backside is facing me, and I'm afraid to turn it over because it's sealed and looks like it's never been opened. How could that be? All the other letters had been opened.

I sit there, staring at it, my body shaking all over. Strange vibrations seem to be floating out from the letter. Quickly I flip it over, but it almost falls on the floor. I catch it, put it right-side up on the bed, and take a look.

Uncle Billy's name is nowhere to be found, or Ann Sweeney's either. I keep looking at the names and addresses, but my brain can't focus.

I pick it up and study it again. Even though there's no PFC William Sweeney anywhere, the handwriting is familiar.

I get out one of Uncle Billy's other letters. It's the same handwriting.

> To:
> Mr. James Patrick Mitchell, Jr.
> 221 Well St.
> Seattle, Washington

"Private James Mitchell, Sr.," is written in the top upper left corner with no address and no postmark or even a stamp. And no censor's initials like on the other letters.

I don't think this has ever been mailed. This is spooky, holding a fifty-year-old letter. Why was it never mailed and how did it end up with Uncle Billy's things? Are James Mitchell, Sr., and James Mitchell, Jr., still alive?

Does Gram know this letter is in here? If she does, why didn't she do something about it long ago? No, she couldn't have known. Gram would have seen that it was delivered to the owner, wouldn't she?

I start walking around the house. Who is James Mitchell? Then it hits me. Where is my brain? Jimmy Mitchell is the dying soldier that Uncle Billy wrote the letter for and promised to deliver. But Uncle Billy must have died before he could do it.

What do I do now? I have to tell Gram about it. But I'm afraid to tell her I opened the box.

Maybe I should just open it and find out how important the letter is. Stupid. Of course it's important. It's the last words of a dying man. And it doesn't belong to me. I can't keep snooping into things that don't belong to me.

But it's right here and nobody's around and maybe his wife and son are dead now, anyway.

Chapter Ten

THE CAR PULLS IN THE DRIVEWAY, and I have to stash the letter. Dad says Gram will probably come home Saturday and that she wants me to visit her tomorrow. Should I tell her all about the box and now this letter?

Dad calls Aunt Rosemary and Tom to invite them over for the weekend. Great. I have this lost letter to figure out, but now I'll have to deal with my nerdy cousin instead.

All night I keep tossing and turning, dreaming about Billy at Jimmy Mitchell's side, writing the letter for him. Then the letter blows out of Billy's hand and into our room, but I can't grab hold of it. It starts flying toward the window and I chase after it, before it disappears forever.

"Carrie, Carrie, what are you doing?"

"The letter, the letter. I have to get the letter."

"What letter?" I'm standing by the window and Molly is shaking me. I start to close the open window. "We have to shut this before it's too late."

"Are you crazy? It's eighty degrees out. Come on. Go back to bed and put on a blanket if you're cold.

"But the let—"

"What's all this about a letter?"

"Just a crazy dream, I guess."

Molly shrugs her shoulder and gets back in bed. So do I and feel better the minute I touch the lost letter, safe under my pillow.

Next thing I know, it's morning and Molly is waking me up again. "What are you doing? I'm not going to swim practice with you."

"I've already been to practice. Aren't you supposed to go visit Gram?"

I look at the clock. It's only nine o'clock.

"Why are you home so early?"

"We have a swim meet tomorrow, so Coach is being easy on us. I've decided to go to the hospital with you. Lisa says she'll drop us off on her way to work."

"Uh . . . I . . ." Think fast, Carrie. She's just trying to be nice. But I have to talk to Gram alone. I have to tell her about the box and the letter and everything.

"Uh, Molly, don't you think it would be better if we spread out our visits to Gram? Then she won't be alone today."

"But I don't want to be the only one with her, in case she dies."

"I know what you mean. But she was better last night, wasn't she?"

"I guess so. All right. You go first. But tell Gram hi for me."

On my way out the door, I remember the locket. I run back to the bedroom and grab the sock from under my pillow, grateful Molly isn't still following me.

As I ride by, Mad is out front watering her mother's garden. What is it this morning? Everybody's on the early-bird plan?

"Where are you going in such a hurry?"

Do I lie? I know she's going to want to come.

"The hospital. Sorry, but family are still the only ones who can visit." Mad frowns. "But Gram comes home tomorrow and you can see her then. Bye."

Mad is going to kill me when she finds out that I've opened the Billy box and never told her, especially now that I've discovered the lost letter.

I pedal furiously for a few blocks but then slow down. What if Gram doesn't forgive me?

The warm sunshine feels good on my sore neck and shoulders. But the air is still cool from last night's rain. I start singing, but I stop. How can I enjoy things when Gram's so sick?

Yet now, when I step into Gram's room, she actually smiles at me. Her eyes don't look so glazed. The doctors say her cancer is terminal. But Gram's strong. She might hang on for a long time and maybe even prove everybody wrong by getting cured.

"Hello, dear. I've been waiting for you."

"Gram, you look wonderful today."

"I am *much* better, thank you. My old hip gave out on me, but that's not going to keep me down. Enough about that. You opened the box, didn't you, Carrie, dear?"

Gram sure didn't give me a chance to work up to it. "I'm sorry. I was just so upset that you're sick and that—"

"—you might never learn my secrets?"

I nod. "How did you know?"

"You asked me about Billy yesterday, remember?"

"I was just going to read one letter, Gram, but when I started reading, I couldn't stop. It was so exciting to learn about your lives during the war." Gram takes my hand. "I found something I think you'd like, Gram." I take the sock out of my pocket and gently pull out the locket.

She takes it from me and holds it in both hands for a minute. Then she stretches the necklace out on the bedspread and looks at it. Finally she opens the locket and stares at it for a long while.

"Is that Uncle Billy, Gram?" Gram nods, then, smiling, she motions me to help her put the locket around her thin neck. "When did Uncle Billy die? What happened to him?" She doesn't say anything. "Why haven't you ever talked about him?"

Oh, lord, I know I shouldn't ask all this. At least not right now. But I have to know. Will Lisa and Molly forget about me, too, when I die?

Gram looks at me with her clear green eyes. No sign of medicine today. "Billy. My dear brother Billy. He died so young. Such a waste of a life." She closes her eyes, and I'm afraid she'd going to fall asleep like yesterday.

But she opens them again quickly. I guess she was just thinking. "My mother was never herself again after that. She died in 1948, five long years after Billy. My father used to say she died of a broken heart."

"Did Uncle Billy die in the war?"

"We used to have so much fun, Billy and I." Gram looks out the window.

"Then he left to fight in World War II, Gram?"

"Not to fight. But he did go."

Just as it appears Gram is going to tell me what happened to Uncle Billy, a teenager in a white jacket with a long brown ponytail brings in a food tray.

"Thank you, dear," Gram says, smiling at him.

When he leaves, Gram turns to me. "My breakfast. They brought me the wrong one an hour ago. I distinctly requested oatmeal last night, not eggs." Now it's my turn to smile. Gram is definitely feeling better.

"But I'm trying to be patient. Everyone makes mistakes." She pours some milk into her bowl of oatmeal and then stirs it around. I go to help her, but she shakes her head.

My heart is pounding. Now that I know Gram's not too mad about the box, I'm afraid she's going to stop talking about Billy.

She eats her cereal for a while and finally says, "He died in Alaska, Carrie, on the island of Kiska in the Aleutian Chain." Oh, no, maybe I'm right.

"Of friendly fire. By his own comrades." Just like Mr. K talked about. "Of course, I didn't find that out until years later. When we were first informed, the officer came to our door and told us that Billy died a hero, helping minister to the wounded soldiers who won back the last Japanese-held island in Alaska."

"He *was* a hero."

"Is a hero killed by his fellow soldiers? Now do you see why I hate war? Gram slams down her spoon, then picks up her napkin and wipes away the lone tear rolling down her cheek.

Will it always hurt, I wonder, losing someone you love?

I go over to hug Gram and want to tell her how Uncle Billy wrote the letter for Jimmy Mitchell, but she starts talking again. "Then when everyone else was celebrating the end of the war, it was bittersweet for us because we'd been a gold star family for almost two years."

"What's a gold star family?"

"Every family that had lost someone in the war was given a gold star to put in their window. Every house that had someone injured in the war had a silver star. There were other homes in the neighborhood with gold stars. Yet somehow another family's grief never makes your own easier."

"How come Dad doesn't know about Uncle Billy?"

"My mother and father never talked about Billy after he died. So neither did I. That's just how we dealt with things back then."

"But the Billy box?"

"I never forgot him, Carrie. I just didn't share my grief with others. Soon after his death, they sent back his medals and letters and other personal effects to us. And when my mother died, I knew my father would never look at the letters, so I brought them with me to Spokane."

"And you never opened the box?"

"No. And I never shared the letters with anyone, not even your grandfather."

"You mean even Gramps didn't know about Uncle Billy?"

"Oh, no, he knew about my brother. But he never met him because Billy died before I even knew your grandfather. Carrie, you have to remember that grief sometimes does funny things to people."

Gram lies back on the pillow. She doesn't look as good

anymore. I've tired her out. But I can't help asking, "Gram, did Billy know someone in the army named James Mitchell?"

"James Mitchell? James Mitchell. I have no idea. But the war brought so many people close."

Gram closes her eyes. As I sit watching her, I feel more mixed up than ever. Uncle Billy died of friendly fire. No wonder Gram is angry. Some stupid American or Canadian soldier accidentally shot him. Is that why nobody talked about it? But he was a hero to Jimmy Mitchell.

Later, biking home, I pedal hard, wishing I could put all this behind me. I want to concentrate on Gram, not some letter written fifty years ago. I'll just get rid of the letter, pretend I never found it. Burn it. Nothing left but little ashes that float away in the breeze. It would be so easy.

But afterward I would feel guilty, thinking about the letter Jimmy Mitchell dictated as he lay dying.

I can't just get rid of it and pretend I never found it. Uncle Billy promised Jimmy Mitchell to deliver the letter in person. I have to do whatever I can to find him. I owe it to Jimmy Mitchell and Uncle Billy's memory and even Gram, in a way.

But what if the letter upsets James Mitchell, Jr.? What if he doesn't want to dig up the memory of his dead father?

When I get home, Molly's eating leftover pepperoni pizza for lunch, so I join her. After an update on Gram, she takes off. Of course, I left out the Billy box part. I hope Gram doesn't say anything to her—then Molly will really be furious with me. She'll say it's another secret. I consider calling Gram but decide not to. Gram will wait until we talk more. She doesn't want everybody to know about Billy, anyway.

Now that I'm alone, I go to our bedroom and find the page where Billy tells about writing the letter for Jimmy Mitchell. That must have been so hard for Uncle Billy. I wonder what it's like to watch someone die.

Uncle Billy must have put it with his things, planning to

deliver it when the war was over. But then he died on Kiska and now, fifty years later, Jimmy Mitchell's letter is still undelivered. I have to find his son. But how?

I must have fallen asleep because I don't even hear Molly until she bursts into our room.

"Letters from a secret beau, Carrie?"

Why can't she mind her own business? And here I thought we were getting along better because of Gram and all. The letters are all over the bed. I try to cover them up with Gram's quilt, but it's too late.

"Whadja hiding, Carrie?" Molly asks, trying to grab a letter.

I start to yell but then stop myself. Molly could blow the whole thing. I take a breath instead and force a smile. "They're pretty special. I thought I'd share them with everybody at dinner, if you could wait till then."

"No. You know how I hate secrets."

"Well, you're going to have to." By now I've moved all the letters under the quilt.

Molly glares at me and then turns on her heel and stomps out of the room. A few minutes later, I hear Mom come in the driveway. The car needs a new muffler. With that roar, I'm surprised Mom's not mortified. But I haven't heard her say a word about it to Dad.

I go out into the hall and listen to Molly whining to Mom in the kitchen about the letters.

"They are her letters, Molly." Score one for Mom.

"That's impossible. There were hundreds of them."

"Oh, honey, they're probably from Sally."

Now why couldn't I have thought of that? No, I have to open my mouth and say I'll share them. And I haven't even asked Gram yet. What if she doesn't want anyone else to know?

I go back to the letters again, but I can't concentrate. Molly's ruined the whole thing. There's no way I can get out of telling the family now. I've got to warn Gram before she comes home tomorrow. I dial the number and ask for room 452, hoping she's not asleep.

She sounds awful, like her voice is coming through a fog. A fog of fifty years ago on the Aleutian Chain. "Yes, tell them. What does it matter now?" Then she hangs up.

Gram, what do you mean? Are you giving up? I throw myself down on the bed and pound the pillow. Why can't I ever mind my own business?

Molly yells down the hall that dinner is ready, and I grab four letters and stuff the rest into the box.

When I finally get to the table, Molly is still glaring at me. Mom hands me a plate of spaghetti and gives me a curious look. Definitely no way out of it now. Yet I feel relieved, too. The secrets are starting to get to me.

We eat in silence for a while. I wish Dad would start his evening ritual of asking about everybody's day. But then I remember it's kind of been dropped since Gram got so sick. I sneak a look at Molly across the table. She's hardly eating. She stares back at me but doesn't bring up the letters.

Finally Dad speaks. "So, Carrie, how was Gram today?" He looks around the table. "Are we all going to visit her tonight?"

"I think she's better, Dad."

"Really?" Dad looks pleased. "That is good news."

"So, Molly, how are things shaping up for your meet tomorrow?"

"Fine. Dad, Carrie has something to share with us all tonight."

Of all nights for Molly not to want to talk about her swimming exploits. I finger the letters in my jeans pocket.

"Dad, are you sure Gram didn't have a brother named Billy?"

"The mysterious Billy again."

"Carrie, just tell us about the letters, please."

I take the four letters slowly out of my pocket and place them in front of Dad's plate.

"Gram had a brother, Billy, who was a medic during World War II. He died of friendly fire during the invasion of Kiska on the Aleutian Chain in Alaska."

"What?" Everyone says at once.

"When I helped Gram clean the basement in her house, we found this trunk. Remember the one that had her dolls?" Everybody nods. "Well, in the trunk there was also a box of old letters that Gram and Uncle Billy wrote to each other during World War II. And that's how I found out about Uncle Billy."

The room is silent. Finally Dad says, "Carrie, there must be some mistake."

"No, look." I pick up a letter and show them the address. "PFC William Sweeney. APO San Francisco."

"Will, how could your mother have had a brother and never told you about him?"

"Gram lost a brother? How horrible," Lisa says, fiddling with her bangs.

They all start passing the letters around and then want more. So I go to my room and get the rest of them, except for Jimmy Mitchell's letter. That's safe under my pillow. Some things are still my secret.

When I get back, Lisa and Molly want to grab the letters from me, but I make them wait until I dole them out, warning them not to get any food on them. Mom suggests we clear the table first.

After reading awhile, Lisa looks up and asks, "So what did happen to Uncle Billy?"

"Carrie's already told us. He died in Alaska during World War II."

"Well, Miss Molly, I learned in history class that no war has been fought on American soil since the Civil War."

"Well, you must have learned wrong."

Here they've just found out about Uncle Billy, an uncle

they never knew existed, and the two of them are arguing about the war. And Dad and Mom don't even try to stop them. They're too busy reading the letters.

I start breathing hard and want to scream, "This is about Gram and Uncle Billy, you idiots, not some World War II history lesson." But I don't. I'm glad they are interested in the letters, but now they're not just mine anymore.

"Carrie, how come you didn't tell us about these before?" Lisa asks.

As I sit there trying to figure out what to say, who should walk in but Aunt Rosemary and my cousin Tom from Seattle. He's gorgeous. What happened to last summer's pimply, shrimpy nerd? The frog has turned into a prince. How and when did this happen?

Tom has the most beautiful brown eyes. How come I've never noticed them before? Lisa runs over and gives him a hug. I guess she notices the difference, too.

I just sit there, staring at him, unable to move. But then Tom and Aunt Rosemary see the letters and start asking questions, so I have to react.

I feel myself losing control. No more secret letters. No more ugly cousin. He's a hunk and he's here, smiling at me. And James Mitchell, Jr.'s letter is sitting under my pillow, waiting for me to do something about it. If only I knew what to do with the lost letter. If only I knew what to say to Tom.

Chapter Eleven

I THOUGHT LAST NIGHT WOULD NEVER END, especially when Mad showed up and my dad invited her in. When she found out about the letters, she gave me this look like, how come I'm the last person to know about these?

Finally, Dad dragged us away from the letters and we all ended up going to the hospital for a while, even Mad. Then Dad and Aunt Rosemary stayed longer while the rest of us left.

We sat around the kitchen eating ice cream and looking at the letters some more until Mad's mom called around eleven and said she had to get home. I offered to walk with her, and when Tom wanted to come, too, Molly and Lisa about fell off their chairs.

On the way back, Tom asked me all about Gram's cancer, selling the house, and Uncle Billy. We walked around the block a few times, and Tom just listened while I told him everything. It felt so good to talk to somebody who cared about what I was going through.

And then, just as we were about to go in, I blurted out about the lost letter. Tom got excited, just like I did, and said he'd help me figure out what to do today.

But this morning he and Aunt Rosemary went to bring Gram home from the hospital—just the two of them, since they see Gram so seldom. And if Gram was up to it, they were going to take her out to lunch, too.

It's one o'clock now. So I guess they went to lunch. I decide to sunbathe in the backyard, but just as I lather myself with sunguard, Mad comes wandering by.

"How come you never told me about those letters?"

"I . . . I was meaning to, but . . ."

"Yeah, right. What a foul-weather friend you are."

"I'm sorry. I just got so caught up in the letters and trying to figure them out. But I did find something else nobody knows about."

When I tell her about the lost letter, her eyes light up. She's happy again. She's my friend and she has a mission.

We go into my bedroom and I show her the letter. "Why wonder about it? Just call the guy."

"Call?"

"Yeah. You might get him on the phone right now. It's worth a try."

She's right. I go into Mom and Dad's room and, picking up the phone, dial Seattle information. "Do you have a phone number for a James Mitchell at 221 Well Street? . . . Are you sure?. . . Well, what other listings do you have for a James Mitchell? Twenty-five? Oh. Could you please give them to me?"

I pantomime to Mad to get some paper. "You can only give me three? Can't you please make an exception this time? This is really an emergency. I have this fifty-year-old letter that's never been delivered and I'm trying . . . Well, could you give me five?" *Click.*

When Mad comes back, I'm standing there with a dial tone. "Maybe I was asking for a lot, but something like this doesn't happen every day."

"You're right. It's such bureaucratic bullshit," Mad says.

"So now what?" I ask, staring at the telephone.

"We open the letter."

"Open the letter? I can't do that."

"Why not? You open everything else, like your grandmother's box." I shake my head. "What's so sacred about this letter?"

"It's not addressed to me."

"You might as well admit that you were born to snoop." I follow Mad back into my bedroom, where she picks up the lost letter off my bed and holds it in her hand. "Maybe there's a clue inside the letter. Did you think of that? Besides, what James Mitchell doesn't know isn't going to hurt him."

She waves the letter in front of my face. "I guess I'll just have to go steam it open myself."

"Give me that letter." I lunge at her hand, but Mad slips out the door like a cat.

"Touchy, touchy," she purrs, as I chase her down the hall.

Bursting through the swinging kitchen door, we run into Gram, Tom, and Aunt Rosemary arriving home from their luncheon. Gram's leaning on her cane, and I almost knock her over.

Steadying her, I almost knock her over again. "Gram, I'm sorry. I'm so sorry. I didn't mean to—"

"Carrie, you've got to be more careful," Aunt Rosemary says, seating Gram in a kitchen chair. "Mother isn't feeling—"

"Stop protecting me, Rosemary. She's just having fun. It's all right, dear. But aren't you going to give me a hug?"

I lean over and hug Gram hard. "Welcome home, Gram. I really missed you."

"Yeah, Gram," Mad says, hugging her, too.

"Hello, dears," Gram says, breathing hard. "These two darlings really wore me out."

"Let's get you settled in your room, Mother, and then you can take a rest."

Gram does look tired. "Maybe you're right," she says, trying to get up. Aunt Rosemary helps her with her cane, while motioning to Tom to carry Gram's small black bag.

"I'm not helpless, Rosemary," Gram says, as Aunt Rosemary leads her out of the kitchen.

"I don't think Gram looks very good, do you?"

"Well, your aunt sure doesn't. She's treating her like an invalid. So what's with the cousin, anyway?" Mad says, pursing her lips and making this kissing noise. I'm about ready to smack her in the face when Tom comes back in.

"What have you guys been up to?" Tom asks.

"Uh . . . nothing," Mad says.

"Right. Nothing," I say, smiling at Tom.

" 'Cuse me, I gotta use the john," Mad says, leaving the kitchen. She turns back to me and purses her lips again but this time without noise, thank goodness.

"Do you want something to drink?" Tom nods, so I get up and pour out two glasses of apple juice, handing him one. "How was the hospital?"

"Harder than I thought. There really is a change in her, more than I realized last night. She seems so frail. I can see why you've been so upset."

"I'm glad she's home. I hated seeing her in the hospital like that. Cancer stinks, you know?" I feel like I'm going to start crying.

Tom grabs my hand. "It sure does." Then he lets it go. "But let's talk about that letter. Have you decided what to do?"

"What letter?" Mad says, barging back into the kitchen.

Tom looks at me. "Ah . . ."

"The lost letter. I told Tom about it last night."

"I thought I was the first one to know."

"You are. Outside the family."

"Some friend you are, O'Leary," Mad says, waving the letter at me as she slams out the back door.

Just then Dad drives up to take Tom, Mom, and me to Molly's swim meet. He won't even let me go find Mad. If she does something to that letter, I'll kill her.

Molly shouldn't even be racing today but Dad says we can't just stop our lives because Gram is sick. Molly, Molly, Molly. The only good thing about going to the meet is that I get to spend more time with Tom. Usually the meets are so boring. How many years have I come to watch Molly swim?

When we get there, I pray that the meet will end soon so that I can get the letter back from Mad. But then Molly swims the 100-meter backstroke and places third in her heat, not even making the finals. I didn't mean for it to get over this soon.

Molly's crying on the way home. Sitting between us in the backseat, Tom says, "I'll bet it's because of Gram. I know emotional stuff like that has affected me before. Two summers ago, when Dad left, I couldn't hit the ball for a month. I think the coach was about to kick me off the team." Molly just nods, but I can tell it makes her feel better.

"I think your cousin's right," Dad says. "Your grandmother's illness has taken a toll on all of us."

I don't want to think about Gram's cancer right now. I have to get the letter back. As soon as we're home, I dash out of the car, leaving Tom standing there. I don't want him to know how stupid I've been.

I ring Mad's doorbell, but she doesn't answer, even when I pound on the door, and say, "I know you're there. Let me in." Where could she be? She never goes anywhere.

Finally I give up and write her a note on the back of an advertisement sitting on the front porch. Then I sprint back to the house and dial her number. The answering machine. "Madeline Connors, if you have done anything to that letter, I will never forgive you. I want it back immediately. Don't you dare even think about opening it. If you do, you're no longer in on the search. Do you hear me?"

Aunt Rosemary's in a tiz when I get back to the kitchen. Just like me. Gram promised to join us for dinner, so Rosemary's cooking a huge Mexican meal—burritos, refried beans, enchiladas. She sends my dad off to the store with a big list, probably not knowing that Gram only eats steamed vegetables.

"Now, Carrie, I want you to encourage Mother to talk about Uncle Billy and World War II at dinner."

"I'll try, Aunt Rosemary. But sometimes she doesn't like to talk about it. It was a really hard time in her life." Aunt Rosemary nods like she's listening, but I don't think she is. She's too busy chopping.

"Now you two get out of here," she says, waving Tom and me out the door.

"Don't you want some help, Mom?"

"No. Go have some fun."

Out on the patio, Tom says, "Where did you go in such a hurry?"

"I had to ask Mad something."

"Well, you sure handled my mother well. She's so pushy."

"You sure made my sister feel better. She never would have listened to me."

"Looks like we've got a mutual admiration society going."

I feel myself getting red. "Maybe we should trade places for a while. Molly drives me crazy."

"Believe it or not, you're lucky having sisters. It's just me and Mom now, and sometimes that drives *me* crazy."

"But you see your dad, don't you?"

"Sometimes, but he lives in Portland, and his new wife just had a baby."

"You're kidding. I didn't know that."

"Mom hasn't told anybody. The idea of my having a half-sister doesn't thrill her too much."

"What's the baby's name?"

"Ann."

"Oh, I love that name."

"Me, too, and so does Mom. She told me she always wanted to name a daughter Ann after Gram. But now Dad has. I guess Stacy's mother's name is Ann, too."

Tom picks up an old tennis ball and starts throwing it against the garage. "I haven't seen your buddy Sally around. How is she?"

"She moved to Vermont last August."

"Ooh, that's rough."

At dinner Mom's face looks kinda pinched, like how much longer do I have to put up with these relatives?

"Mother, are you up to saying grace?"

"Of course," Gram snaps. Why is she so touchy with Aunt Rosemary? "Bless us, O Lord, and these thy gifts which we are about to receive from thy bounty, through Christ Our Lord. Amen. Thank you, Lord, for this family that takes such good care of me, and in your infinite wisdom please guide us in all your ways."

Aunt Rosemary brings Gram her special dish of steamed vegetables and rice. Guess I was wrong. I know this macrobiotic meal is supposed to help Gram's natural healing, but it looks so boring compared to my plate of spicy Mexican food.

Before Gram can even start eating, Aunt Rosemary blurts out, "So, Mother, tell us everything there is to know about Uncle Billy. I can't believe you've kept him a secret all these years."

Gram doesn't say a word.

"Gram, just tell us a little about World War II, like you did before," Lisa says, touching Gram's arm. I smile at her. Sometimes she knows just what to say. *Sometimes*.

Gram takes a few bites and then starts talking. "Well, appreciate what you're eating because during the war, every American got a ration book that had point coupons to be turned in for scarce items such as sugar, meat, and gasoline. We had to choose what we wanted very carefully and pool our points in the family. I always turned my book over to my mother. It was amazing how she could stretch things."

"Were ration books like getting welfare, Gram?"

"Oh, no, Lisa. Our family was never on welfare."

"Tell us about the letters, Mother," Aunt Rosemary says, sounding frustrated.

"Well, I wrote letters every week to Billy and other family friends. We all did. And I knitted scarves for soldiers at the Red Cross every Saturday afternoon.

"What I really wanted to do was to meet some handsome young soldiers, but your great-grandfather wouldn't dream of letting me go down to the canteen to help out. Ooh, I was so mad." Lisa looks over at Dad, and they both start laughing. They're always arguing about curfews.

"Finally, when I turned eighteen Mother let me sneak out some evenings. I worked at the Saint Mary's Service Center on Mondays and Wednesdays. On Friday evenings I sold coffee and donuts at the Red Cross canteen located in the Ferry Building. But by then, Billy had died and it wasn't as much fun as I had hoped."

Gram stops and gets this faraway look, like she's forgotten we're in the room. She tries to take a drink of water, but her hand is shaking too much.

Later, when Gram goes to bed, my sisters, Tom, and I play kings in the corner in the kitchen while Mom, Dad, and Aunt Rosemary talk in the living room. It's fun being together. I feel more comfortable with my sisters when Tom's around. Like he'll stick up for me if things get heated.

Suddenly Lisa throws down her cards. "I can't understand why Gram never talked about her brother. It's sad." She turns and looks at me and Molly. "You'd better not forget me when I die. I want you to mention my name ten times a day, do you hear me?" she says, poking her manicured nail into my chest.

"Don't joke, Lisa."

"I'm dead serious, Carrie."

"Very funny, Lisa," Molly says.

"No, Lisa's right, Molly. I just hate it when adults sweep problems under the rug. Do you know my mother never mentions my dad's name? Here they were married for fifteen years, and now it's like he never existed. After I come back from a visit with Dad, she never even asks about him."

"Maybe it hurts too much, Tom. It must be really hard that your dad's new wife just had a baby."

"Uncle Ted has a new baby?" Molly shrieks. "I didn't know that. How come you didn't tell me that, Carrie?"

"Because I just told Carrie today. Mom hasn't told anybody. She acts like it never happened."

"Just like Gram didn't talk about Uncle Billy? Can sorrow do that to a person?" I ask.

"Not me. I'm going to talk about the people I love forever," Lisa says.

"Gram was going to take us all to California this summer, Tom. Said she'd always wanted to show us where she grew up. But now . . ."

"Enough, Carrie," Tom says, getting up and going outside. "Why does everybody have to be so negative about everything?"

"What's with him?" Molly asks, as I get up.

Lisa grabs my arm. "Wait, Carrie. Give him some time alone. He's just getting used to the idea of Gram being sick."

"But he likes to talk to me."

"Oh, I think Carrie's got a crush."

"Cut it out, Molly," Lisa says, then smiles at me. "But you have to admit that he's gotten awfully cute. I just wish Aunt Rosemary were half as neat as Tom is good looking. You should see the coffee stain she left on my dresser. I don't see why they have to sleep in my room while I get stuck sleeping on the floor in yours."

"Poor Lisa," Molly says, looking at me. "She never gets what she wants."

"I know. But she's such a slob, Carrie. And Tom's things are all neatly folded in his suitcase."

"That's probably why Uncle Ted divorced her."

"Molly, what an awful thing to say. People don't get divorced over neatness, at least I don't think they do. Well, at least my husband won't have to worry about that," Lisa says.

"Stop it, you two. Aunt Rosemary isn't herself. She's upset about Gram." How did I end up defending Aunt Rosemary?

"She's not the only one," Molly says, wiping away tears.

Is this how it will end? All of us crying over Gram? Unless I find James Mitchell . . . Where is Madeline?

Chapter Twelve

I NEVER FOUND MAD last night. Instead, I dreamed that the lost letter was ripped into shreds and strewn around my bedroom. But when I wake up, the carpet is clean. I see a note from Mom that she, Dad, and Aunt Rosemary have taken Gram to early mass, so I get the Sunday paper off the front porch. There, sitting on top, is a manila envelope addressed to me. Inside is the letter with a Post-it note attached: "Sorry I got you so worked up. Why don't you trust me more?"

Tom is second up, and I start to show him the letter until Molly barges in. I leave instead and deposit it safely under my pillow.

When I come back, I'm surprised to hear Gram talking. "Not long after V-E Day, my sister Rose and I went to a ceremony at the Civic Auditorium. My parents weren't up to it. We listened to speeches and sang 'God Bless America' and 'The Star Spangled Banner' with the only military band they could round up."

"Mother, would you mind if we videotape this? They're such wonderful stories."

"No, Rosemary. I look awful and I . . . Oh, why am I telling these stories anyway?" I can see Dad shaking his head at Aunt Rosemary in the background.

"Go on, Mother. I'm sorry. It was a silly idea." Aunt Rosemary looks like she's going to cry, but when Gram starts talking again, she takes out a notebook and starts writing instead.

"Well, most of the soldiers weren't back from the war yet. I remember the flag unfurling and the crowd clapping and clapping. Then they started reading out the San Francisco boys who had died. We kept listening for Billy's name, but we must have missed it. The place was so packed and noisy."

Gram stops and takes a sip of juice. "And then in June 1945, San Francisco was chosen for the first session of the UN. I was thrilled it was happening in my own city and that I was chosen as a representative from Notre Dame Academy to be an usher."

Gram moves her eyebrows up and down, her eyes dancing. "I wore my little uniform—a one-piece dark navy blue serge. It had a bodice to the waist and a pleated skirt and I wore a clean white blouse with a stiff point collar. Oh, we looked sharp."

I always thought wearing uniforms would be a pain. But Gram makes it sound great, and it sure would take care of the worry about clothes.

"I was part of it all. And I was so deeply proud. Stalin, Churchill, and Roosevelt were meeting at the War Memorial Opera House, and somehow I believed they would figure out how war would never happen again. But it hasn't turned out that way, has it?"

"I'm never going to war, Gram," Tom says.

"I'm not, either," I say. "It's horrible."

"Well, I hope *none* of you go. Now all this talking has worn me out. Tom, why don't you walk me around the block? I've got to get used to this old thing." She points to the cane and rolls her eyes. Dad and Aunt Rosemary look so happy when she says that.

I get up to clear the table. Out in the kitchen, Tom tells me to come along. I shake my head. Tom deserves some time alone with Gram before they drive back to Seattle today. "But I thought you wanted to tell her about the lost letter."

"I don't know how she'll react."

"Do it now. Before I leave."

"When you get back," I whisper, just as Molly comes through the swinging door.

"What are you two whispering about?"

"About what a good-looking woman you are, Molly."

"Stop it," she says, snapping me with a dish towel.

I'm waiting in Gram's room when they return. Tom helps her into bed, and then we both prop her up with some pillows. She's still smiling, so, taking a breath, I lay out the letter in front of her on the bedspread and tell her I found something else in the Billy box.

Hands shaking, she holds the envelope up to her face and squints. She's always been farsighted. "I don't understand, Carrie. Who are these people?"

I tell her all about James Mitchell, and she studies the envelope again.

"Look, Gram," I say, "it's never been mailed."

She takes a gasp of air and says, "Now I remember—the young soldier who was dying. You mean his letter was in that box all those years and never delivered?" I nod my head. "You must read me Billy's letter where he talks about Jimmy Mitchell." I squeeze Gram's hand. "And most importantly, Carrie, you must locate the owner of this letter."

Tom gives me the thumbs-up sign while Gram studies the letter again. "I guess I never found this letter because I just couldn't face going through Billy's things after he died."

Aunt Rosemary calls down the hall. "Tom, are you ready to go?"

Why do they have to go so soon? Aunt Rosemary is always rushing things.

"Good-bye, Tom, dear. Have a safe trip. You're such a dear boy. Thanks so much for coming to see me." Tom hugs Gram. "Help Carrie here find the owner of the letter, won't you?" Gram's voice starts to fade. "I think I'd better rest now."

"Of course, Gram," Tom whispers.

In the hallway Tom hugs me and says, "What did I tell you? Now remember—I'll do anything I can to help. Why don't you send a letter to James Mitchell at his old address?

Maybe he still lives there." All I can do is nod. So many things to think about.

"Tom, why don't you stay for a few days and help me? Your mom won't care."

"Oh, yes, she would. She gets lonely when I go out on Friday night." I never thought of Tom going on dates. Of course he has a girlfriend—he's so good-looking now.

"Besides, I've got my lawn jobs, remember? But we'll be back. Maybe next weekend."

Mad comes over the instant she sees their car pull out. "So where's your cute cousin?"

"Liar. You were peeking out your front window, just waiting until he left."

"It must be hard to see the man you love drive away like that."

"Shut up."

"Why did you tell him about the letter before me?"

"Why did you steal my letter?"

"It's not your letter, and besides, I returned it in perfect condition. I needed to teach you a lesson because you were getting so hyperactive about the whole thing."

"I've got to deliver it the owner. I promised Gram."

"You told her?"

"This morning."

"With Tom, I suppose?"

"Oh, stop being so jealous. He's my cousin, for Pete's sake. Maybe if I find James Mitchell, Junior, Gram will get better."

"I don't think life always works that way, Carrie. But it's worth a try." Mad lies down on the lawn in the front yard and looks up at the blue sky. I sit down beside her. There's hardly a cloud in the sky.

"You could just write 'please forward' on it and stick it in the mail, with current postage, that is."

"I've thought of that. But what if it gets lost? I can't afford to take the chance."

"Well, don't send the real letter, then. Send another one that tells about the lost letter."

"Yeah, that's what Tom— I mean what a terrific idea. You are really smart, you know that, in some things, worldly things, I mean."

I run into the house to get some paper. While rummaging in the kitchen junk drawer, I hear Mom and Dad talking in the dining room. "Will, I hope we can handle it when things get really bad."

"We'll bring in outside help, if we need to."

"I worry about how the girls will take it."

"They're tougher than you think. What about you? I know it's going to disrupt the household even more than it already has, but I can't let my mother die in the hospital."

"Of course not. But all these visitors. Rosemary said she might come every weekend. Maybe they should stay in a hotel next time."

I run back outside, afraid I'm going to start yelling at Mom and Dad. Gram dying? Tom in a hotel?

Outside I don't talk to Mad. Instead, I start writing really fast, then crossing out and changing words around. Finally I'm satisfied with it. When I look up, Mad's staring at me. I'd forgotten all about her.

"You're amazing. Whenever I have to write in school, I just freeze up. But you were going a mile a minute."

"I just had something I needed to write, that's all."

"Let me see it," Mad says, ripping the paper out of my hand. She's such a pushy broad.

June 26

Dear Mr. Mitchell,

My name is Carrie Ann O'Leary and I found this letter addressed to you in our basement in a box of my great-uncle

Billy Sweeney's things from World War II. I'm sorry it was in my uncle's box all these years, but my gram was too sad to ever open the box up. Now she's really sick with cancer, and so I finally opened the box and found a fifty-year-old letter I think your dad wrote to you during the war. I hope you are still alive and not upset that you didn't receive it long ago.

You see, when your dad was dying on Attu, he asked my uncle to deliver this letter to you in person, but then my uncle died in the war, too. I guess they put the letter in with all his other things, and that's how it ended up in the box. I'm sorry about all this. Please call or write me if you are the James Mitchell who had a father who died on Attu during World War II and you want the letter.

I called Seattle information and you don't live at that address anymore. But I'm hoping the letter will get forwarded to your current address. If you're not still alive, maybe one of your relatives would want the letter. I would appreciate it if you would write me back and tell me about yourself. I hope you like the thought of getting a fifty-year-old letter from your father.

Sincerely,
Carrie Ann O'Leary

"Wow. Do you lay on the syrup or what? It makes me want to cry." Mad pretends to wipe away tears, and I try to punch her, but she moves away. "Really, it's great. Just the right tone. No spelling mistakes or anything. At least that I can see. I wish I could write like this, but nobody's ever taught me."

"Do you think it's ready to mail?"

"Perfecto."

"All right. Give it to me and I'll go type it."

"I wouldn't. Old snoopy Molly's around. Why do you have to type it, anyway?"

"Because I want it to seem official. Not just from some jerky kid. Do you have a computer?"

"No, a typewriter. Mom's still living in the ice age."

"Yuck." But in the spirit of secrecy, we go over to Mad's and I type while she reads the comics. When I'm finished, I want to mail it, but then I remember it's Sunday.

"Let's bike to the post office," Mad suggests. "They have a Sunday pick-up."

"How do you know?"

"Didn't you say I have street smarts?"

Chapter Thirteen

IT'S BEEN OVER A WEEK since I mailed it. Enough time for a letter to get to Seattle and back to Spokane if James Mitchell, Jr., isn't at that address. But no word.

It seems like Gram's gotten worse. Just days ago, she talked quite a bit. But now she stays in her room, reading Billy's letters, talking to friends on the phone, or just sleeping. She says she's too tired to read books or watch television, though last night she did watch the fireworks from our porch.

Gram used to go to the park all the time to feed the ducks, before all this cancer business. So I got a brainstorm to take her back up to the South Hill to Manito Park. Lisa said she'd come home on her lunch hour to drive us, and when Molly heard about it, she even got out of swim practice early so she could come, too.

Now, sitting at the picnic table eating the fried chicken and brownies Molly and I made last night, it feels great—except that we had to stop three times from the car to the picnic table so that Gram could rest.

These cute guys are watching some girls playing softball,

and they end up flirting with the outfielders. Seeing them laugh and fool around makes me wish I hadn't quit the team.

Lisa starts asking Gram about her old boyfriends, but Gram only wants to talk about Gramps and Uncle Billy. The minute she starts talking about them her face looks younger, and the dark circles under her eyes seem to disappear. "I met your grandfather a couple of years after the war was over—1947, I guess. Plenty of handsome soldiers still around, but until I met your grandfather, nobody could take the place of Billy. They both had dark, curly hair and fair Irish complexions and were as fun as could be. Though there was a bit more of the devil in Billy."

Gram laughs. "The girls were crazy about Billy. Maybe because he never acted full of himself."

Molly offers Gram a brownie. "Thank you, but it's not on my diet," Gram says, delicately taking a piece of green pepper out of the plastic bag. Always a perfect lady. "It feels good to be out, girls. Thank you. Say, did Carrie ever tell you about my taking you to California?"

Lisa and Molly eye me suspiciously. "No."

"Well, so much has happened lately. When I get better, we're going to California. I want to show you girls where I grew up."

"Oh, Gram, that would be wonderful," Molly says, hugging Gram.

"That's settled, then. We'll definitely go in August." Gram closes her eyes and takes a bite of her pepper, while we all look at one another, wondering if the trip will ever happen.

"So, Gram, *how* did you meet Gramps?" Lisa asks.

"Well, he stayed in the army after the war and was stationed at the Presidio in the city. I met him at a dance at Saint Mary's Service Center. I was working as a secretary then, helping support the family."

"How did your parents like him?"

"Very much—until we were married and he dragged me to Spokane, away from my family and friends."

I had never thought about how Gram might have missed everyone when she moved to Spokane. Like my missing Sally, but probably much worse.

After Lisa drops us off and we get Gram settled in her room, Molly attacks me in the kitchen. "How come you never told us about this trip to California?"

"I did. When Tom was here." Molly shakes her head. "Oh, I guess we were too upset about Gram then."

Suddenly Molly looks like a scared little girl. "Carrie, do you think Gram's going to get better? She seemed better today, don't you think?" My throat chokes up and I can't answer. So I just shake my head, not sure if I'm nodding yes or no.

Dad got mad when he heard we took Gram to the park. Didn't he hear us talking about it at the dinner table last night? Sometimes I think he's only half here. He told Mom she should have stopped us, and Mom said, "They're responsible girls. They've been taking very good care of your mother, Will. I'm afraid you just want to keep her all cooped up in this house, as if that will help her get better."

"That's exactly what I had in mind." Mom looked at him as if to say, well, it's not working.

But now this morning I wonder if we should have taken her out. She looks horrible. Her face has that gray look, like the ashes in a campfire, all burned out. I walk around her room, rearranging the books and picking dead flowers out of the vases. Then I sit down and look through her pile of get-well cards.

> I love you, Ann. Fight hard. Get well. You can beat this.
>
> Lillian

Take good care of yourself, Ann. You are stronger than any cancer. You are a survivor. Call us anytime.

Love,
Dorothy and John

Since Gram doesn't want many visitors, everybody just keeps sending presents and cards. I used to be jealous Gram had so many friends, especially last fall after Sally left, but Gram always made time for me.

I watch Gram sleeping. Her skin is so dry I could peel it off in one piece. Why didn't I notice that yesterday? And she looks so thin. Mom's always trying to get her to eat.

Gram wakes up and calls out. "Water. Water." I sit her up in bed and pour her a cup. Then I hold it to her lips. How can this be the same woman who was laughing in the park yesterday? Was it just a dream?

"Thank you. That tastes good. Carrie . . . Carrie."

"Yes, Gram?" I try to sound normal. That's what Mom says to do. Just be myself. But what if being myself means crying?

"Why aren't you out having fun on such a wonderful summer day?"

"Because I want to be with you. We had fun yesterday at the park, remember?" Gram smiles. "Molly left a note that Tom called this morning." Gram frowns. She thinks long-distance phone calls are a waste of money and that it's a shame the art of letter writing has been lost.

"Gram. He called before eight on the cheap rates. He wanted to know how you were doing and said to tell you he missed you." I'll bet he was also bummed out that I didn't answer the phone so he could ask about the lost letter. Can I help it that I'm a night owl and sleep in late?

"I'll bet he wanted to know about that lost letter."

I nod. Sick or not, Gram still doesn't miss a trick. "Gram, I'm going to find James Mitchell. You're going to be so proud of me."

"Carrie, I've always been proud of you. Don't you forget that. But I am glad you are trying to find that boy. It should have been taken care of long ago."

When Molly gets home from swim practice, we offer to take Gram out in the backyard, but she says she's not up to it. Is it her body or her mind that doesn't want to move?

I have to get out of her room. After a few hours, I start feeling claustrophobic, like if I don't get some fresh air, I'll suffocate.

I go over to Mad's, and she's in her backyard sunbathing, wearing orange and hot pink patterned shorts with a moonglow green tube top. Very subtle.

I look at my freckled, chunky legs. They look absolutely thin compared to hers. But not as thin as Gram's, poking out from the white sheets on her bed this morning.

"They say we'll probably all eventually get cancer, at the rate the world's going."

"Well, aren't you the happy camper this morning?"

"Would you be? Gram looks awful today. And how am I going to find James Mitchell if he's not at that address or the letter doesn't get forwarded? I mean, if there was a letter floating around out there for you that was fifty years old, wouldn't you want to get it?"

"Depends. If it's a bill, no thanks."

"It's not funny."

"I know. My mom never laughs when she gets a bill." Maddie rolls over on her back.

I bend down and tap her on the shoulder. "You don't seem to understand. This is James Mitchell, Junior's last communication from his dying father. Wouldn't you want a letter from your father, no matter how old it was?"

"I don't have a father, remember?"

"Everybody's got a father."

"A biological one. Mine ditched me before I was even born." Mad rolls over and sits up. "At least nobody can say my looks scared him off."

"I'm sorry. I guess I figured you saw him sometimes."

"Nope, you could say I don't have much of a family life."

I stand there thinking what it would be like to live just with my mom. No sisters, cousins—at least I've never heard Mad talk about cousins.

"Cousin. Tom. That's it. Tom could send us the twenty-five addresses from the Seattle phone book."

"Tom again. Aren't you giving up a little soon? Maybe it's in JM II's hands this very instant."

"Then why hasn't he called me?"

"Because it's only been nine days. You're obsessed, do you know that? All you talk about is Gram, Tom, Uncle Billy, and James Mitchell."

"Because that's all I think about," I say, lying down on the other chaise lounge. "Do you have some sunscreen?"

"No. The point is to tan, Carrie."

"But I don't tan, and I don't want skin cancer when I'm older, especially with my genes."

"Does Lisa diet all the time? She's got such a good figure."

Funny. I didn't think Mad even cared about her weight, like maybe she'd just given up or something. Is that all anybody cares about—looks? Even Fatty Maddie?

"Kind of."

"In case you haven't noticed, I eat all the time."

"So do I, except when I went on that macrobiotic diet with Gram."

"I remember when you were really thin like Lisa."

I get off the chaise longue and leave Mad's yard without a word. Does she say those things to make me feel bad or does she just have a big mouth?

When I get home, Molly's sitting on the patio. "How's Gram?"

"Sleeping."

"She doesn't look so great today, does she?"

"She was fine yesterday in the park."

"Temporary." I go over and put my hands on Molly's

shoulders. "I'm telling you now, as my next of kin, that when it's my time, I want to go fast, no life supports or anything. I'll probably never marry and Mom and Dad might be dead and Lisa will be living in Paris with some artist. So it's up to you."

"Carrie, stop," Molly says, moving away from me. "You're scaring me."

I follow her. "Do you think cancer is hereditary, Molly? Are we all going to get it, too? If so, I'm scared because I could never stand the pain like Gram. I'd be crying all the time." Molly hugs me hard until we both get embarrassed and I go inside to check on Gram.

Later, when Molly goes to the mall with her friends, I sit with Gram, watching out the window for the postman. When he drives up, I quietly leave the room and run outside. It's there. The letter I sent to James Mitchell, Jr., stamped ADDRESSEE UNKNOWN.

I knew this would happen. I knew it couldn't be as easy as sending it to that old address. So now what? Tell Madeline. No, I'm mad at her.

But she shows up before I've even gone back into the house. I hand her the letter without a word.

"So now the real work begins."

"Right. What?"

"Get the Seattle Mitchell addresses from Tom."

"Oh, so you're actually speaking the *T* word now without choking?"

"Don't be joking with me, girl."

I go into the house and call Tom. I don't care if it's the middle of the day or not. I don't care if Dad screams and hollers when he gets the bill. He won't mind when he finds out about this letter.

Tom answers the phone on the first ring. I can't believe it. Just luck that he's home on a lunch break from his lawn jobs. He says he'll fax the addresses over on his Mom's machine at work when he picks her up tonight. But where should he send them? Mad quickly scribbles down a number and hands it to me—the fax number at the art gallery where her mom works.

When I hang up, I say, "Way to go."

"Thanks."

"But are you sure that's the right fax number?"

She gives me a dirty look. "I thought you trusted me."

Do I?

Nothing to do but wait until tonight, so Mad and I go sit with Gram for a while. Mad is hesitant going in. I guess she hasn't seen Gram since she got so sick. I push her through the door and then point to a chair.

Mad stares around the room with this weird look on her face until Gram sits up at one point. "Any news?"

"Gram, the letter came back addressee unknown." Gram's lips start to quiver. "But don't worry. Tom's going to send me all the Mitchell addresses from the Seattle phone book so we can track the owner down that way."

"Oh, I'm so glad Tom's helping you."

"I'm helping, too," Mad says. "We're using my mom's fax number to get the addresses."

Gram nods. "That's nice, dear." I wonder if Gram knows what a fax number is or even cares.

When she's asleep again, Mad and I go into my room to rewrite the letter but end up arguing about whether to say we have a letter from fifty years ago or not. "You'd better be careful. The wrong person might get ahold of this and want to cut in on the action."

"What action?"

"Like a fifty-year-old letter might be worth some money, especially from a dying soldier. Everybody's out for a buck nowadays. Just tell them you found some old letters of your great-uncle Billy's from World War II on the Aleutian Chain and that you want to learn more about how your uncle died.

Then say the letters mention a Jimmy Mitchell of Seattle and that you're trying to locate him so you can find out more about your uncle."

"But we know that James Mitchell, Senior, isn't alive, and that information might not be enough incentive for his relatives to want to write back. I have to mention the letter. That's the hook. Even if it's risky, I can't take the chance his son won't be interested enough to contact me."

"I don't know."

"Mad, we're running out of time. You saw Gram. We have to move on this right now." Mad nods. "Wait. I know. I'll go ask Mr. Kingston what to do. Will you stay with Gram?" Mad looks at me, like okay, but what if something happens? "It'll be fine. I'll just be down the street."

I grab the lost letter and a couple of others and run over to Mr. K's. First I tell him he was right about the friendly fire and that Uncle Billy did die that way. He gets this real sad look in his eyes. Then I show him the lost letter and he's as amazed as I was at first. "But how do I find this James Mitchell?"

Mr. K thinks a minute, then asks if he can see the address on one of Billy's letters. After he studies it a moment, he calls information, asking for the number of Fort Lewis in Tacoma.

"If I want to find one of my old army buddies, all I have to do is contact a public affairs specialist at Fort Lewis, and they'll locate his current address. Maybe we can find Mr. Mitchell this way."

My heart starts to beat quickly when Mr. K picks up the phone again. Maybe he's right. Any moment now we might find out where James Mitchell lives and then I can deliver the letter. Gram is going to be so happy.

"Oh, I see. But isn't there some way you can trace the . . . I understand. Thank you anyway."

"It seems they don't keep track of the next of kin once the soldier has died, especially from fifty years ago."

I feel the tears well up in my eyes. We were so close.

Mr. K puts his arm around me. "Don't you worry, Carrie. We've only just begun to fight. I have lots of friends in the army, some from my Alaska days and some further up the line. You leave it to me. I'll find that address for you."

Chapter Fourteen

WHEN I GET BACK, everything's fine. Mad and Gram are even laughing. How come Gram doesn't laugh with me?

Mad doesn't seem that interested in leaving the room, so finally I have to drag her into the hall. "Don't you want to know what happened?"

"Well, I can tell by your face that Mr. K didn't have any bright ideas."

"Huh. Mr. K's got friends in the army and he's going to go all the way to the top to get the address." Mad rolls her eyes. "Well, he did serve in Alaska during World War II, you know." Mad still doesn't look impressed. "He also said that it can't hurt to write all the Mitchells in Seattle."

"We'll have to work on the letters at my house."

"When my parents get home, I guess. I can't leave now."

"Go over without me. I'll stay with your grandmother."

I don't think I want to be in Mad's house all by myself, and besides, I've hardly been with Gram all day. But just as I tell Mad she'd better go, Dad comes home and sees us standing outside Gram's door.

At dinner Dad explodes. "Only family can visit Gram. What's going on here? Trips to the park, Madeline coming over. Don't you realize how sick she is?"

"But she still has to live, Dad," Lisa says. "It's like a morgue in her room."

"Your mother and I have been talking, and we've decided that we need some extra help taking care of your grandmother. We're asking too much of you girls. So, a hospice worker is going to visit Saturday, and we'll see how she can help out."

"I can take care of her, Dad. I don't want some stranger coming in and taking over."

"Carrie's right," Molly says. "She does a really good job with Gram, and I can help more during the day."

"I'll cut my hours at work, Dad, so I can be around more."

"No. It's too much for all of us. We're getting help. She's coming and that's final."

Great, I think, walking over to Mad's after dinner, strangers in our house. I can't believe Mom is putting up with all of this. She's always been so possessive of the house, never even wanted a cleaning lady.

When I get to Mad's she's out on her front steps waving a piece of paper—the Seattle addresses. I walk inside, where her mom is reading the newspaper. "Thanks, Patty, for getting the fax."

"No problem. Glad I could help out."

I'm surprised she doesn't ask me about what we're doing. Does Mad have too much freedom? If my parents knew, they'd be all over me, wanting to know everything. But then I remember they don't know anything I've been up to lately.

I revise the letter on Patty's electric typewriter, which has been set out on the dining room table for me. Mad doesn't sit and watch this time. Instead, she stays in the kitchen and argues with her mom about who's going to do the dishes. I wish I could do this at home on our computer, and then Mom could help me proofread it. But I've gone too far on my own to blow the secret now.

I finish up and reread the letter, hoping I sound halfway intelligent. I don't want the people receiving this to think it's some kind of practical joke.

Patty reads it over and says it's great. Then she offers to drop us off at the copy place while she goes grocery shopping.

When we get there, we make twenty-five copies and one more for my files. And while we're waiting for Mad's mother, we decide to buy some envelopes and start addressing them.

We split up the list, but then I notice Mad is writing really messy. "Come on, Madeline, this is important. I don't want them to think I'm some slob."

"Are you saying I'm a slob?"

"No, it's just that . . ."

"Listen, Miss Perfectionist. The point is to get them written so the postman can deliver them, right? At the rate you're going, your grandmother will be dead before they get in the mail."

My pen stops in midair and the woman at the next copy machine looks over at us. "I don't believe you just said that. I thought you were sorry she was sick. Well, you're the sicko now." I stand there, trying not to cry.

"Come on. I'm sorry. I don't know why I said that. I'm such a jerk sometimes."

I pick up the letters and envelopes and start walking down the street. Mad follows me.

"Carrie, I'm sorry. Come on. Stop. My mom won't know where we are."

"I'm walking home. You finally blew it this time. I'm doing it all myself now."

"No, you aren't." Mad grabs the papers out of my hand. Some rip, and others just fall on the ground.

I start to kick her and hit her. She just stands there and takes it. "I'm sorry. Me and my big mouth."

I'm crying now. "I have to do this right, at least one thing right for Gram."

"You're doing everything right for her."

"No, I'm not. I hate being in her room. I hate seeing her suffer."

"But you still go in there. No one wants to watch someone they love die. Most kids would have bailed out long ago. But not you. You sit with her day and night."

"It doesn't bother you."

"Sometimes it does and, besides, she's not my gram."

Mad's mother drives up next to us and honks the horn. Mad waves at her, then stoops down and picks up the dirty letters off the ground. "Why don't you get in the car? I'll be right back."

When Mad returns, she climbs into the car and hands me a stack of new letters. And then she says, "Mom, I think this would be a perfect time to go have some ice cream."

"Madeline, your di—" she says, looking around at us. "All right. That sounds like a good idea. Carrie, why don't we stop by and pick up your mother?"

I never would have expected it, but when we get to my house, my mother practically jumps into the car. I think she and Dad were talking about Gram again when I walked into the kitchen. Molly and Lisa are home, too, and they want to come. Lisa never seems to go on any dates anymore.

Dad just says, "Go, go." So we all go, cramming into Patty's old station wagon. Lisa gets in front, and Molly motions for me to squeeze in the back between her and Mad.

As we drive along, Mad says, "Remember those house tours we used to go on?"

"Yeah," Molly says, "with the moms gabbing in the front and us fighting in the back." We all laugh.

"I still haven't gotten my dream house, Susan. How about you?"

Mom shakes her head, laughing, or is she crying?

Later, when they drop us off, Mad grabs my arm before I can get out of the car. "I'm really sorry for what I said about Gram. Am I still on the project?" I nod, watching Molly and Lisa walk up the sidewalk. Is it time to tell them?

When I check on Gram, Dad's in her room, dozing in the chair. I go to our room and start addressing envelopes and stuffing letters in them. If Molly finds out now, she finds out. But she's on the phone in the kitchen.

When I finally finish, Molly's still talking on the phone and Lisa's bedroom light is off. I read for a few minutes, but then crash. I'm so tired lately. But tomorrow I'll mail the letters and the big wait will begin.

Time drags by. Four, six, now eight days since I mailed the letters. It's been harder waiting than I thought it would be because everybody's so down in the dumps around the house—except for Lulu. Yes, Lulu, Dr. Gonzales's nurse, volunteers for hospice in her free time. I can't believe it. She's around sick people all week, and now on Saturdays she does more of it.

I just about died when she showed up last Saturday. I answered the bell and Lulu just said "Hi" and plowed through the door. This time she was wearing bright yellow sandals and a hot pink short outfit. I think she and Mad must support the same fashion designer. I knew she looked familiar, but finally it was the clothes that tipped me off.

"I remember you. You work at the clinic."

"Yes, and you are Ann's granddaughter." She didn't waste much more time talking, even when I told her Mom and Dad would be home soon. She just wanted to know where Gram's room was.

She said hello to Gram, then immediately moved her into the chair so she could change the sheets, all the while chatting away. Then, when Gram said no to a sponge bath, Lulu convinced her that it would make her feel better. Mom had been trying to get Gram to take one for days now.

When Mom and Dad got home from shopping, I thought surely Dad would ask Lulu not to come back after he heard how loud and noisy she was. But instead, he seemed so relieved when Lulu said she'd be back again next Saturday.

And now today, Saturday, something much better has happened. Yes! I got a response. Not one, but two. I call Mad before I even open them, and she comes running right over. I watch her out the window. Is she losing weight or do I just like her better now?

But then we open them—two negatives. Neither had heard of a James Mitchell, Jr., or Sr., and didn't have any relatives who fought in Alaska during World War II. "Sounds interesting," one man wrote. "Hope you find him."

Mad insists on reading them again out loud. Then she starts analyzing their handwriting and trying to figure out what they might look like. Why bother? I think. Nothing else matters except that they said no.

Gram's the same today—no better, no worse. When Lulu shows up, I introduce them, and I can tell Mad likes her. Mad gets this glint in her eye that says, hey, this lady's cool.

But Lulu doesn't stop to talk. She wants to see Gram right away. Mad goes home, kind of hurt, I think.

Lulu and Gram talk for a minute, and then Gram asks if it's time for her pain medicine. Lulu looks at me, and after I check the clock, I nod. Lulu nods back, so I pour out the pills and hand Gram a glass of water. But I don't want to watch while Lulu rubs Gram's throat so she can swallow the pills. I go to the kitchen. A few minutes later, Lulu comes to find me.

"Is there any chance Gram's going to get better?"

Lulu puts her arm around my shoulders. "Carrie, with brain cancer it's not humanly possible that she will recover.

With a lot of cancers, you can remove the malignant parts and use chemotherapy or radiation to prevent the spread of the disease. However, your grandmother's cancer is too far gone."

"But she was fine at the park last week."

"I know. Sometimes they go into remission and then later take a turn for the worse."

"Why didn't they catch it before it got so bad?"

"We thought we were monitoring it well enough. But sometimes a patient can be fine one month, and the cancer have spread like wildfire by the next checkup."

"It's not fair."

"No, it's not. We can pray for a miracle. But maybe it's your grandmother's time to die."

"I don't want her to die. But she's in so much pain all the time. Should I hope she dies soon so she won't suffer so much?"

"Just pray. And let the Lord decide the rest. I know the hardest part is watching helplessly as a loved one suffers. The best thing you can do is be with her so she's not alone."

I haven't done much praying lately. I'm pretty mad at God.

Three more negative letters come in the mail with no comments or anything. Except for one woman—at least it looks like a woman's handwriting—who wrote, "Good luck, honey. I hope you find him. I'll be praying for you."

That makes me feel better. But Mad just laughs—says she's probably some wacko who contributes to those preachers on TV. Can't we take anything on face value anymore?

Gram's having another bad day. I gave her a foot massage, but it didn't seem to help. She's thrown up twice in the last hour and asked at least twenty times for her pain med. Then she says she wants to get up and use a real toilet. So I unplug the catheter from the bag and help her out of bed. Even though she's so thin now, I still can't handle her alone because her arms are so weak that she can barely hold on to me.

I want to help her by myself, but I can't, so I sit Gram on the bed and rush into the kitchen to see who else is around. Mom's just gotten home from work; she puts her briefcase down and follows me.

When we come into the bedroom, all Gram will say is "bathroom." We walk her slowly down the hall and into the bathroom. Lulu arrives just as we're getting Gram back into bed. She comes by some evenings now—just seems to pop in whenever we need her most.

I guess Lulu can tell I'm pretty upset. She walks me to the kitchen.

"Gram keeps getting worse and worse. A person shouldn't have to suffer like this. She doesn't even seem like my grandmother anymore."

"I know."

"There must be something else we can do. Sometimes when I go in to say good-night, her eyes are moving really fast back and forth and she looks scared."

"The nights are always the most difficult time."

Mom comes into the kitchen, looking tired and drained but still healthy, with such pretty, young skin. I think of Gram's face and shiver.

"Your daughter and I were just talking about how the nights are the roughest time for Ann."

Mom nods. "For all of us, I guess."

"Are you and Dad staying up with Gram at night? I didn't know that."

"Sometimes."

"Well, I'm going to do it from now on. I don't have a job or anything else to get up for in the morning."

Lulu pats my arm. "No, Carrie. That's too much for one person. But maybe you could all trade off sleeping in her room. That way she'd always have somebody with her."

I can't stand to talk about it anymore so I go back to Gram's room. Mom and Lulu talk for a long time in the kitchen.

At dinner, when Dad hears about our conversation with Lulu, he's not happy. "Why was Lulu telling a thirteen-year-old girl that? Carrie needs her sleep."

"Because Carrie asked. She's with your mother more than anybody, and she notices these things."

Dad lets out a sigh. He looks tired, too. "I guess I should have noticed it myself." Dad turns to me. "It's a very thoughtful idea, honey. Thanks for taking such good care of your grandmother."

"I help, too," Molly says.

"Of course you do. Everybody's been helping." Dad looks around at all of us. "I know it's been hard. I'll sleep with Mother tonight."

Everybody starts talking at once. Lisa says, "We could put a fold-up cot in there and take turns. I'll sleep with Gram the night before my day off."

"And I can do it when I don't have early swim practice."

Part of me wants to be the one with Gram all the time. But part of me knows I can't stand it sometimes. Ever since Gram got really sick, I've known that Gram needs me. But now I'm learning that she needs all of us to make her journey.

Chapter Fifteen

WHAT A BAD DAY. Aunt Rosemary just called to say they won't be coming over next weekend—car trouble. I wanted to see Tom so much. And then the mail—two letters today. All from people who know nothing about the Mitchells. Eight total now. It's been too long, and I've pretty much given up hope. I told them in the letter that it was really important that they get back to me right away, even calling collect if they had to. I know that was risky and Dad would have a fit. But just one call is all it would take to find the right owner. And Dad would understand when he found out what this was all about.

But no phone calls. And no wackos wanting money either. At least Mad was wrong about that.

I guess a few more could come in. But I doubt it. Gram's going downhill fast. She's in a wheelchair now. The cane wasn't enough for her. If this is going to help her, I have to find JM II now. But what if none of James Mitchell's family lives in Seattle anymore? Everybody moves around nowadays. James Mitchell could be anywhere in the country—or the world, for that matter.

Mr. Kingston's not having any luck, either. Yesterday he was really down when he told me. Usually he's Mr. Smiley.

Mad comes over while I'm fuming in the kitchen. I give her an update and she says, "Maybe we need to send letters to other towns in the state of Washington and around the United States."

I run into the living room and bring back the atlas. We flip open to Washington State. There are hundreds of towns.

"Check the Spokane phone book," Mad says, shoving it toward me.

Why didn't I think of that? James Mitchell could have been living in this very town the whole time. I scan through the Mitchells, my hand shaking. "There are three!" I yell out, just as Molly walks into the kitchen.

"Three what?"

"Ah . . . Three guys I like!"

"There are?" Molly says, staring at me. "Who?"

Trying to keep my voice steady, I say, "Do you think I would dare tell you? You'd blab it to all your friends."

"And Madeline won't?"

Mad looks at Molly with a straight face and says, "None of my friends would be the least bit interested." Molly sighs and leaves in a huff.

Mad and I look at each other and start laughing. "So tell me, Carrie, who are these guys?"

"I thought your friends wouldn't be interested," I say, laughing again. "Hand me the phone."

I check the phone book again and begin to dial—534-5226. *Ring, ring, ring*. "Hello. Is this the Mitchell residence? Is James Mitchell there? Oh, I see. . . . Well, do you happen to know if his father served on the Aleutian Chain during World War II? . . . But did he go to Alaska? . . ." I hang up the receiver and start rubbing my ear.

"What happened?" Mad says, pulling on my arm.

"She's divorcing James Mitchell because he's a drunken bum and so is his father. They're probably out drinking right this minute and would I please leave her alone."

I take a breath and pick up the phone again and dial while Mad calls out the numbers. I get one "no longer in service" and one no answer.

"Oh, what's the use? What are the chances he moved from Seattle to Spokane? He could be in Florida, Japan, Greenland. I'll never find James Mitchell, Junior."

"Maybe you won't. But nobody can say you haven't tried."

The next day I'm upstairs reading one of Gram's old letters when Molly comes bursting into the room. "Who is this from?" Molly asks, shoving one of the letters at me.

Cripes, I missed the postman. "You are so nosy," I say, trying to grab it from her, but she holds on to it.

"Who is James Mitchell?" she asks, waving it around.

I jump up and try to get it from her. But she pulls away. "None of your damn business." I lunge again, and this time my hand gets part of the envelope, but then it rips, half in my hand, half in hers. "Give it to me. Give it to me," I scream. "This could be it."

I run into the kitchen and grab some tape. I lay the two parts of the letter out on the table and try to put it together, but the tape keeps mangling. Molly gets a scissors and, cutting off a piece of tape, hands it to me.

Shaking, I read the patched-up. Negative. At least this should have been it, the one worth spilling the beans for.

"You have no business looking at my mail."

"Why are you getting letters from strange men? I'm going to tell Mom and Dad."

"Go ahead. I'm going to have to tell now, anyway."

"Tell me first, please. You've been acting so weird lately. Ever since you found those World War II letters. Does this have something to do with them?"

How does Molly know? Oh, what does it matter now? Maybe she'll even have some brilliant idea about how to find James Mitchell, Jr.

No, I might as well tell the whole family at once about the letter search and what a bust it's been. It'll give me a chance to call that one last Spokane James Mitchell a few more times.

"I want to tell the whole family together—at dinner."

Molly stomps her foot. "You always say that. Come on. I'm your sister. Tell me now."

"No."

"Is Mad in on this?" Molly asks.

"Yes." No use hedging now.

"I thought so. You two have been acting so suspicious. I guess you trust her more than me."

"All right. All right." I tell Molly the whole story of the lost letter, but it takes me a long time because she keeps asking so many questions. Afterward she's so happy. She even helps me cross off the most recent rejections from my list. I still haven't heard from nine of them.

Finally Molly goes in to visit with Gram, and I'm left in peace. I bring the phone into our room and call the last Spokane number. Twenty-five rings—still no answer.

Not wanting to lose my nerve, I take the lost letter out of my pocket the minute everybody's seated at dinner and pass it over to Dad. Then I tell the story, talking really fast and showing them the Seattle addresses and responses and everything. Molly sits there smiling, thrilled she was in on the secret, if only for an afternoon.

"Our chatty Carrie has been keeping all this to herself?" My mother sounds surprised, but not upset. "No wonder you've been acting so skittish lately, always wanting to check the mail."

"We could have helped you, Carrie," Lisa says, studying the envelope. "I wish you had told us sooner."

"I was going to, but then I decided I wanted to succeed on my own. But now that I've failed, I could use all the help I can get."

Mom looks at me. "Why, Carrie, you haven't failed. You've acted like a real detective, following every lead."

"Yes, Carrie. I'll bet you find this man very soon."

"But what do I do now, Dad? Contact all the James

Mitchells in the world?" Dad sits thinking, as he takes a bite of his hamburger.

"We'll help you think of something," Molly says. They all nod.

"So you're not mad at me?" I look around the table.

"You would have shared it eventually, wouldn't you, honey?"

"Of course, Mom."

"Let's pray." Dad bows his head. "Dear Lord, thank you for this meal and for all our blessings. Thank you for Carrie bringing back some of our family history. Help her find James Mitchell so he can have back part of his father. And finally, help my mother endure the pain that's been asked of her." Dad's voice chokes on this. "Amen."

Gram. In all this letter talk, I'd forgotten Gram.

Tonight it's my turn to sleep with Gram. She sits up when I walk in wearing my pj's and gives me a tiny smile—like it would hurt for her to smile any more than that. Then she falls back against the pillows and shuts her eyes. I stand next to her bed, wanting to rip her eyes open.

Gram and I haven't talked for several days. I wanted Mad to come over so we could tell Gram funny stories about getting the letters back and calling the Mitchells. But she's out of it now. I don't even think she'd know what we were talking about.

It's stupid for me to be worrying about that letter all the time. It's not going to make Gram better, and there's still so much I don't know about her. I wonder what she thinks about when she closes her eyes or if she thinks at all.

Molly comes in to say good-night and I whisper, "Doesn't she look awful?"

Molly just nods. Then Gram opens her eyes. "Water. Water." I can barely make out what she is saying. Then, when I finally do, Molly has already poured a cup and handed it to me. I hold the cup to Gram's lips, but she can only takes a couple of sips. She's having a lot of trouble swallowing.

"Pat?"

"Gramps isn't here, Gram."

"Who are you?"

"Carrie. Carrie. I love you, Gram. I love you, Gram." I sit on the bed and hug her, her bones so fragile in my arms. After a while, Molly pulls me up and walks me over to the cot.

She gets me to lie down while she sits in the chair and keeps me company. Gram is making these low, moaning sounds, but finally her breathing quiets down. I doze off but then wake up with a start.

Gram is sitting up in bed and has pushed off her covers. She throws her legs over the side of the bed, looks at me, and says, "Well, Carrie, let's get on with it!"

"With what, Gram?"

"Locating James Mitchell. Don't you think that's what Billy would have wanted?"

"Oh, yes, Gram. But what do I do next?"

"Why, go to Seattle, of course. That's where the letter belongs. We'll go to Well Street and see if we can find any old neighbors. And if that doesn't work, we'll start knocking on the doors of all the Mitchells who didn't answer your letter." I close my eyes and shake my head. Is Gram suddenly better? But when I open them, Gram is sleeping. She doesn't look in any shape to go to Seattle. Okay, Gram, I guess it's all up to me.

In the morning when Mom comes in, I feel stronger than I have in several days.

"Mom, do you think Gram's well enough for me to go to Seattle?"

"Seattle . . . what are you—?"

"I know. You can't believe I would leave her like this. But Gram told me in a dream last night that we should both go to Seattle to find James Mitchell. Since she can't go, I have to do it for both of us."

"Carrie, I don't want you going on some wild-goose chase around that big city."

"Mom, don't you understand that this search is giving Gram something to live for?"

"Honey, she has all of *us* to live for."

"I know, I know. But Uncle Billy meant so much to her, and she didn't deliver this letter that was in his box and now I'm going to do it for her and then she's going to get better."

"Oh, honey." She gives me a hug. "I'll have to talk to your father."

No letters in this afternoon's mail. When I come in, Molly's fixing a p.b. sandwich. She asks how it went spending the night in Gram's room, and I tell her about the dream.

"You should go. Definitely. I was thinking of that myself."

"Really? Mom didn't seem too positive about it this morning."

"Call Tom. Maybe he can get Aunt Rosemary to invite you over."

I dance around with Molly. "That's it." But then I stop. "Mom and Dad will know I set it up."

"Who cares? Getting there is what counts."

"But what if Gram dies while I'm gone?"

"She won't die until you've found James Mitchell."

"Then maybe I'd better not find him."

"I didn't mean it that way, Carrie."

"How will I get there?"

"The dog, of course."

I call Tom before dinner, and he says he'll start working on his mom right away. I tell Molly, and we decide I should wait until Aunt Rosemary calls before I tell Dad, unless Mom spills the beans first.

But everybody's distracted at dinner, and before I know it, Aunt Rosemary is on the phone. When Tom says he'll do something, he does it.

After Dad hangs up, I can hear him and Mom talking in the kitchen. Suddenly he swings open the door and practically knocks me over. "Hi, Dad."

"Well, did you miss any of the conversation?"

"Dad . . ."

"Aunt Rosemary invited you to spend a few days in Seattle. Any special reason?"

"Don't be mad. I just have to find James Mitchell. Gram told me to do it."

"Well, then, you'd better do what she says."

"Thanks, Dad." I'm shocked. He never gives in this easily.

"Thank your mother; she's been your real supporter." I run over and hug Mom. "Your mother thinks you are old enough to take the Greyhound bus alone to Seattle, and I do, too. But to tell you the truth, I'd kind of like to help you find this James Mitchell, so I've decided to take Friday off work and drive you to Seattle. I figure the weekend would be a good time to contact people."

"But, Dad, I wanted to do this—" Mom shakes her head at me, as if to say, Take what you can get, Carrie. I'm disappointed I can't go by myself on the bus, but she's right. I'm lucky to be going at all.

Dad keeps talking as if he hasn't heard me. "Why don't you go get all your notes and addresses so we can go over them and make sure this trip doesn't turn out to be some half-baked affair."

I start to leave the kitchen, then stop and turn around. "Thank you, Mom and Dad. This means a lot to me and Gram. Could I sleep with Gram again tomorrow night?"

"Sure," Lisa says, walking in with a stack of dinner dishes, "but you get the floor." She gives me her wicked smile. Is that what drives the guys wild?

The phone rings, and it's Madeline. She's going to want to come to Seattle, too. What am I going to tell her?

Chapter Sixteen

THIS AFTERNOON Mad came over to say good-bye. She was quiet, not acting like herself at all.

"I wish you could come. You've helped so much."

"Are you crazy, man? Your Aunt Rosemary is not exactly wild about me."

"She's been going through a rough time lately, with the divorce and Gram and everything."

"She could still be polite to people."

"Well, maybe she's afraid you're out to snag her son." Mad laughs—a little too hard, I'd say. Does she have a crush on Tom?

"I'll call you the minute I know anything."

"Or I might call you. Give me your cousin's number." Oh, no. Is she going to start calling Tom?

At dinner Dad wants me to practice what I'm going to say when I ring these strange people's doorbells, but I can't do it because Molly keeps making faces at me.

After dinner everybody sits awhile with Gram. Finally, around ten-thirty, I roll out my camping pad and sleeping bag and Lisa turns off the light. We lie there in silence, listening to Gram's breathing.

"Carrie, do you ever worry that the next breath might be her last?" I nod in the darkness. "When I'm in here alone, I keep watching her, praying her chest keeps moving. Sometimes I'm afraid I'll be the only one with her when she dies."

"I know. Molly said the same thing. It makes me not want to go to Seattle."

"You have to go. I just wish Molly and I could come with you."

"Well . . . Maybe you should."

"Don't be silly. This is your thing." Lisa doesn't sound jealous, more like wistful.

"Mom says I should tell Gram I'm leaving. But how? When I talk to her now, I don't even think she's listening."

"Tell her, anyway. Somewhere deep in her heart she'll hear you."

I've been asleep for a while, an hour or two maybe, when I hear Gram call out Lisa's name. We both wake up and stumble to either side of her bed. She keeps asking for something, but we can't understand her.

Her brow is wrinkled in frustration, and her tongue is so swollen that she can't form her words clearly. She keeps trying to say something, but we don't know what.

Then suddenly, like an old frog, she croaks, "Guess." We don't get it at first. But she keeps saying, "Guess, guess, guess."

I look at Lisa and say, "Let's make it a game. Water, Gram?" She shakes her head no.

"Bed up?" Again no.

Then Lisa tries. "Bed down? Hair combed?"

"Legs rubbed?" Come on, Gram. It's gotta be something. I start laughing. This is absurd. "How can we play a game when we don't even know the rules?"

Gram seems to like that comment. A smile at the corners of her mouth starts moving up her face. "Bathroom? Food? Music? Read?" She shakes her head no at everything.

We run out of ideas and start repeating them. Then Lisa practically shouts out, "Pray!"

Yes! Gram finally nods yes. Finally we get the right answer, but what do we pray? The Our Father? Hail Mary?

"Let's just take turns saying whatever comes into our heads." Lisa nods and points at me to start.

"Dear God, thank you for giving us Gram. Help her get better if it's your will and if not, at least help her with her pain because, God . . ." I can't go on.

"Help Gram on her journey and help us know how to help her on that trip." Lisa's voice is quiet but strong. "And finally, Lord, help Carrie find James Mitchell. Amen."

"Amen," I say, ending with the sign of the cross.

I take Gram's hand. "I'm going to Seattle tomorrow, Gram. I'm going to find James Mitchell." I'm not sure, but I think she squeezed my hand before she closed her eyes.

When she's sleeping comfortably, Lisa and I go to the kitchen to make hot chocolate. "The praying really helped, Carrie. We should try it more often."

When the h.c.'s ready, we take our cups and go sit in the living room. "Gram always knew what to say to make me feel better. Remember my first middle school dance last fall? I had such a horrible time that I came home and cried in my room."

"I remember. I tried to tell you how much I hated middle school dances, too, but you didn't believe me." I look at Lisa in the moonlight. She's so pretty.

"Well, it was hard to believe, coming from Ms. Social. Anyway, Gram came to talk to me. She didn't mention the dance, just said that boys didn't really take a shine to her at my age. She said she was skinny and little and a late bloomer, like Dad, and that only her mother told her she was pretty."

"Gram said Dad was a late bloomer?" Lisa says, wrinkling up her nose and laughing.

"Yeah, she said he couldn't believe it when Mom, such a good-looking woman, went for him. Before that, he was too busy studying or working on cars to even date."

"So Mom was a hot ticket?"

"Yep. Just like you, I guess."

"Gram is beautiful, and you're going to be beautiful, too, Carrie. Sometimes I get worried because I've heard the pretty girls in high school lose their looks early and that the most attractive girls at the high school reunions are the late bloomers."

"Lisa, you are going to look gorgeous forever. It's actually kind of disgusting," I say, sticking out my tongue at her.

We go back into Gram's room, and just as I'm about to close my eyes, I whisper, "Lisa?"

"Yeah?"

"Sometimes I worry that when Gram dies, I'll forget what she looks like."

"So do I, Carrie."

Lisa and I both wake up early, surprised that in spite of the guessing-game episode Gram seems to have slept pretty well. Dad joins us in the kitchen soon after and happily says, "Everything's all set, Carrie. I've even got a few business calls set up in Seattle this afternoon. We can go on the JM II search tomorrow, and then maybe Tom and Rosemary can drive back with us on Sunday."

I still wish I were going alone on Greyhound, but beggars can't be choosers, I guess. I wanted to do this on my own. But up to now, I have. At least having Dad along makes me not so worried about Gram. She wouldn't die with both of us gone. Would she?

Driving along through the wheat fields of eastern Washington, Dad starts talking about how Gramps always wanted to be a farmer.

"Really? I could see Gramps that way, but I never pictured Gram as a farmer's wife."

"Well, she wasn't as crazy about the idea. But Dad could never get the capital to buy a farm, anyway. He was a good worker, though, a damn fine one. And would have made a great farmer."

Dad takes out a pack of gum and offers me one. He's been chewing gum ever since he quit smoking five years ago. Then he starts humming along to "Dock of the Bay" on KXLY, the sixties station he always listens to. "I don't know about me. I was always better at selling raffle tickets or Camp Fire mints for Rosemary than digging dirt."

People have always told me what a persuasive salesman Dad is. I close my eyes and try to imagine Dad as the top raffle ticket seller in his high school or messing around under his car or flirting with my mother at the peace march. But I can't. He's just my dad.

A long time later, I wake up and Dad says, "Thanks a lot, kid. Here I thought you'd be keeping me company." My head is full of thoughts, but nothing comes out. Instead, I look out the window at the mountains and tall evergreens. I can smell the change in the air. We're almost to Seattle, where, hopefully, somewhere James Mitchell, Jr., is this very moment waiting to hear from me.

"You know, Carrie, I admire your curiosity about history and people. You sure didn't get it from me. I'm much more comfortable with things."

"I guess all this reading about World War II has kind of made me wish I lived back then."

"Really?"

"It just seems like people were more united and concerned about one another. Nowadays it's just everybody out for themselves, no matter how it hurts other people or the earth."

"Whoa. It wasn't that simple, Carrie. We put off joining the war until the Japanese bombed Pearl Harbor. We didn't want another war. Twenty years before, we'd just fought World War I—the war that was supposed to end all wars."

"Huh?"

"Huh is right." Dad lets out a sad, frustrated laugh, then

steps on the gas pedal. "Maybe there weren't as many protesters then as during Vietnam, but there have always been people against war."

Dad drops me at Tom's around one and takes off for his appointments. Tom has two more lawns to do before dinner, so I go with him and help, raking, trimming the hedges, and unloading the clippings.

I like working with Tom. He laughs a lot and never criticizes. But he doesn't look quite as handsome today. More like a cute cousin. Maybe he was in some kind of rosy glow at our house.

At dinner all Dad and Aunt Rosemary talk about is Gram. It makes me sad to think about her, so I leave the table and Tom joins me in the living room. We go over my list and try to make a plan. Before dinner I had called the remaining names on my list, but just got negatives, no answers and two no longer in service. Suddenly I get the sinking feeling that this trip is a colossal waste of time.

But then Tom suggests we all go to a movie, and I'm surprised when Aunt Rosemary and Dad agree. It isn't quite a date, sitting between my cousin and my dad, especially when Dad is laughing like a goon at Robin Williams. But it's the closest I have ever gotten to a date, and I do like sitting next to a boy in a movie theater.

Chapter Seventeen

I TRY THE PHONE NUMBERS AGAIN this morning, but no luck. After studying a Seattle map, Tom figures out where Well Street is located, and Dad drives us over there. Somebody on the block *has* to remember the Mitchell family.

I'm starting to get excited now. I love driving around Seattle, with the Space Needle always on the horizon. When we get closer to Seattle Center, Tom leans over and says that he'll take me there if we have time.

When we get to Well Street, hardly anybody's around except for a couple of kids on trikes and a teenager lounging on a porch. They won't know the Mitchells. But then my dad thinks to ask the teenager if any older people live on the block. That's it. All we need is to find another Mr. Kingston.

"Yeah, there's some old guy that lives down at the end of the block."

We park the car and get out. Walking up the sidewalk, I'm suddenly nervous. This is crazy. But then I notice that the house is old and big and has a swing, just like Gram's, and I'm not so nervous anymore. Dad waves for me to knock, so I do. Inside the screen door this old geezer type is sitting in a white undershirt watching wrestling on TV.

"What do you want?" he shouts, not even bothering to come to the door. My dad motions me to talk.

"Hi. I'm Carrie Ann O'Leary from Spokane, and I'm trying to locate a James Mitchell, Junior, who used to live here on Well Street with his mother fifty years ago during World War II."

"What?" This time he gets up out of his chair and comes to the door.

"Hello, sir. My name's Will O'Leary, and this is my daughter Carrie and my nephew Tom Christenson."

Finally the man smiles and steps onto the front porch. He sticks out his hand, and he and Dad shake. "Jim Randall. So just what are you up to, young lady?" He doesn't seem so weird anymore.

I tell him the story of the lost letter, and he gets very interested. "I was born in this house. Lived here seventy-eight years . . . Mitchell. The name sounds vaguely familiar. What was the address?"

I take out the letter, my hands shaking. "Two twenty-one."

"Well, let's walk over there. It's across the street and down three houses. "The Phillipses live there now. Young family that moved in last year. They're on vacation right now, but I don't think they'd know anything, anyway. The house has changed hands a lot. Hmmm . . ." Mr. Randall stands there staring at the house for a long time.

"I think my wife knew a Mrs. Mitchell whose husband was killed in the war. I was off in France then. And when I got back, they didn't live here anymore."

"Well, could your wife help us?"

"Afraid not. She's been dead for fifteen years." My heart sinks, and my face flushes in embarrassment. Tom takes over for me.

"Oh, I'm sorry, sir. Is there anyone else on the block who might remember?"

"Nope. I'm the last old-timer."

Mr. Randall invites us back for ice tea, but I can't even taste it. What are we going to do now? Drive around to all those addresses where the people didn't even bother to answer my letter?

Tom calls his mother but then hangs up the phone quickly. "Uncle Will, we have to get home right away. Aunt Susan called right after we left, and apparently Gram took a terrible turn for the worse this morning. The doctor isn't sure how long she has now."

Dad drives like a speed demon over the hills. At the house, Aunt Rosemary is standing in the driveway with her bags already packed. Dad gets out and hugs her, but she pulls away.

"Where have you been for the last two hours? I didn't know what to do, except pray that you would call."

"I'm sorry, Aunt Rosemary. We were—"

Dad waves me to hush up. "Rosemary, why don't you take a plane? We can drop you at the airport on our way out of town." She shakes her head. "All right, then, both you and Tom fly over."

"No, I already checked into it. It will take almost as long for me to go to the airport and catch the next available flight to Spokane as to drive. Besides, I need your company right now," Aunt Rosemary says, looking around at us. "Mother will hang on until we get there. She has to."

"Tom, go upstairs and get packed." But Tom just stands there, like he's in shock. Aunt Rosemary pushes him along. "All right. I'll help you." I follow them into the house, needing a glass of water.

"Pack your suit. You might need it."

"Mom, I hate that suit. It's way too small. I keep telling you I need a new one."

"Don't blame that on me. If your father weren't so tight with his money—"

"Mom, not now. Not again."

I run out of the house, crying. Why all the arguing? Gram's dying. And all this time I kept fooling myself that she would get better if only I could find the owner of the lost letter. Who was I kidding? That stupid letter means nothing. Staying alive is what counts.

Dad comes over and puts his arm around me. "Why does Gram have to die? Why couldn't we have found James Mitchell? That's all I wanted to do for her."

"Hey, don't give up on either one yet. Come on, grab your bag and get in the car. Your grandmother is waiting for us."

Tom brings his Walkman along, but neither of us feels like listening to it. Nobody feels like talking, either, so we just drive along in silence with Tom and me in the backseat, munching on granola bars.

When we drive through Snoqualmie Pass, Tom finally says, "I once promised Gram that I'd take her downhill skiing."

"Like you took me? You'd better not. That was awful, ditching me on the hardest slope and then the ski patrol having to come and help me ski down." Tom starts laughing, and I glare at him.

"I still haven't forgiven you." This was a couple of years ago, when he was a nerdy shrimp. Amazing what a little maturity and weights can do.

Aunt Rosemary cries for a while, but then she perks up. "I can't imagine Mother downhill skiing. Not after all her fits when we went skateboarding."

"You two skateboarded?" Tom and I both say at once, laughing.

"I thought they didn't have skateboards back then."

"They certainly did, Miss History. I'll bet if you look through those boxes again, you'd find my old one. Did you hold on to yours, Rosemary? You always were gutsier than I was."

"Do you think so?" she asks, punching Dad on the arm. "You never told me that before."

What will I remember about when I was growing up? Gram's cancer?

After a while, I fall asleep and dream about a man in a uniform, carrying a baby. The baby won't stop crying, no matter what he does. Finally the soldier hands the baby over to this pretty woman and walks backward, waving good-bye, good-bye, good-bye.

Then I hear Gram calling me through a fog, like Dorothy at the end of *The Wizard of Oz* when her Aunt Em is calling her home.

"Gram, Gram. Are you still alive?"

"Carrie, I'm free now. I'm going to see Pat and Billy and my parents. Don't worry about me and I won't about you because I know you'll find the owner of the letter."

"Really, Gram? How? When?" But before Gram can

answer, I wake up. Tom's asleep beside me. Dad and Aunt Rosemary are talking quietly up front.

Gram has died. Should I tell them? I look at my watch—6:30 P.M. I read once that when people die they appear once more to their loved ones before going to heaven.

"Dad? I just had a dream about Gram."

"Did you? Well, we're almost home. Right near Cheney, only about twenty miles now."

I want to tell Dad about Gram. But I can't. How do I know for sure?

When we get home, I'm the first one out of the car. Mom comes out to meet us. "Is Gram still alive?"

"Yes, honey." I let out a big sigh, and Mom hugs me hard. "It's been a rough twelve hours, but she's hanging in there."

"I have to see her right now."

"Why don't you let your father and Aunt Rosemary go in first?"

"But she might die any moment. Maybe she's already dead. I have to see her."

"We can all go in together, Susan," Dad says, giving Mom a hug. "Isn't there anything else that can be done for her?"

"The doctor says the cancer has totally taken over her brain and that all he can do now is try to control her pain with drugs."

"Should we put her in the hospital?"

Mom shakes her head. "There's nothing they can do for her there, and she wants to die at home."

Dad walks slowly into Gram's room, as if he's afraid of what he'll find in there. So am I. Molly and Lisa are standing around the bed with Lulu.

Gram's eyes are all glazed over, her chest hardly moving. Her right arm has fallen limp beside the bed, while her slim left arm lies still on the blanket. I can hardly stand to look at her.

We sit quietly with Gram, and then Father McCann arrives. For some reason, Gram kept putting off having the sacrament of the Anointing of the Sick. But tonight she told Mom she was ready.

"May the peace of the Lord be with you always," Father McCann says, as he sprinkles Gram with holy water.

We answer, "And with you, too."

Then Dad reads from the Bible. "The Lord is my shepherd; I shall not want. In verdant pastures he gives me repose . . ." I've always loved that passage. I feel better.

Father McCann does another Scripture reading about healing the sick, and then we leave the room while Gram confesses her sins. When we come back, Father anoints her forehead with the oil of chrism and says, "May the Lord in his love and mercy save you and raise you up."

After more prayers, we all say the Our Father together, and then Gram gets communion. I feel really peaceful the whole time. Gram looks peaceful, too, her face calm and relaxed.

After Father leaves, we sit with Gram some more, but she soon falls asleep. So Dad sends us to bed and says he'll wake us if anything changes.

I can't sleep. Molly and Lisa are snoring away, but I keep wondering if I'll ever see Gram alive again. I wish Dad had let me spend the night in her room. If only I'd found James Mitchell. Maybe it could have made a difference.

Later I wake up sweating, and I don't even have a blanket on. Sneaking down the hall, I tiptoe into Gram's room. Aunt Rosemary and Dad are both asleep in their chairs. But Gram's eyes are open. I go over to the bed and take her hand. "I love you, Gram. I love you so much." She nods and closes her eyes.

Afraid it's her last breath, I lean down into her until I can feel the locket move up and down on her chest. She's still breathing, but her lungs are so congested. Lulu said cancer patients often die of pneumonia because their lungs fill up with fluid.

I study her face. She looks a little better this morning. Maybe the anointing helped, and she's recovering. Stranger things have happened.

Sitting on the bed, I keep holding her hand. It's going to be all right. She's still alive. I can find James Mitchell today. I can call those Seattle numbers from here. And that Spokane number I haven't been able to reach.

"Carrie, I want you to have this locket when I die."

"Gram, I don't want you to die. Aren't you afraid?"

"Not now, not after last night. Father told me that when God reaches out his hand, you can take it when you are ready. I'm ready, Carrie."

Gram closes her eyes again, but she's still breathing when I hug her.

After a while, I feel Aunt Rosemary shaking me awake. "Honey, why don't you go get something to eat?"

I look down at Gram sleeping peacefully, and I don't feel so sad. How can this be?

Seven thirty A.M. on the kitchen clock. Nobody else is up. It's probably too early to make phone calls, but I pick up the phone anyway and start dialing one of the Seattle numbers. It's not too late. As long as Gram is alive, it's not too late.

No answer.

Next number. Five rings. I'm just about to hang up when a quiet woman's voice answers.

"Is this the James Mitchell residence?"

The woman hesitates, then answers, "Yes. What do you want?"

I take a deep breath. "I hope I'm not calling too early, but I just had to call you today. You see, I've been trying to contact you for a while now. My name is Carrie O'Leary, and I am looking for a James Mitchell, Jr. Did you get my letter explaining the situation?"

"No. But I've been gone for two months and just got back last night. I haven't even looked through the mail yet."

"Oh." At least it isn't no. I explain to this woman about the lost letter written by James Mitchell, Sr., in Alaska during World War II to his son, James Mitchell, Jr., on Well Street in Seattle.

"Oh, honey." The woman's voice sounds so sad. "I can't really make sense of what you're saying right now."

"Oh, I'm sorry. I must have waked you up."

"No, no. It's all right. It's just that I'm James Mitchell III's wife. But he died two months ago in a motorcycle accident. We'd only been married a year. So I have no idea if his grandfather served in Alaska."

"Oh, I'm sorry. I'm so sorry to bother you."

"Not at all. But I think you want James Mitchell, Junior."

"Yes, whose dad was James Mitchell, Senior."

"So you need to contact my father-in-law."

"Does he live in Seattle?" I can feel my heart start to beat faster.

"No, they live on Whidby Island now."

"Is James Mitchell, Senior, still alive?"

"Jimmy's grandfather? Oh, no. He died during World War II, but I don't know where."

"So could I call your father-in-law to find out if he's the owner of this letter?" The woman hesitates. She must think I'm crazy. "You see, my gram is dying of cancer, and I promised her I'd deliver this letter to the right person."

"Oh, my . . . I'm so sorry your grandmother is sick. I know what it's like to lose somebody you love."

"Maybe you should call your father-in-law and explain everything first."

"All right."

"And then I could call you back so you don't have to pay for a long distance call."

"Here's James Mitchell, Junior's number—206-779-5889—just in case." I write it down carefully and read it back to Mrs. James Mitchell, III. "Now give me yours. I'm sure my father-in-law will want to talk to you. If you don't hear from him soon, go ahead and call him."

"My number is 509-747-0906. Oh, and the address on the letter is 221 Well Street. Thank you, Mrs. Mitchell. Thank you so much."

"Carrie, I hope it *is* Jim's letter. He could use some good news. We all could. By the way, my name's Christine. Christine Mitchell."

"Good-bye, Christine. Thank you again. I'll be waiting for a call." I hang up and feel like dancing. For the first time, I really feel like I might have found the owner.

I fix myself a bowl of cereal and try to stay calm. It's only eight o'clock. I shouldn't have called that woman so early.

"Who were you just talking to?" Tom sure looks good in the morning.

"How's Gram?"

"Mom's with her. She actually looks better today."

"I know. I thought so, too. Maybe she isn't going to die. Tom, oh, Tom, you won't believe what just happened."

"What?"

"Yeah, what?" Molly says, walking in. I tell them about Christine Mitchell and all the Mitchells.

"Who is Christine?" Lisa says, joining us.

"Christine Mitchell. She's married to James Mitchell, III, whose father is James Mitchell, Junior, and whose grandfather is James Mitchell, Senior," Molly tells her.

"Wait a minute. Who's Christine's husband?" Lisa asks.

"James Mitchell, III, and James Mitchell, Junior, is her father-in-law," we all say.

"Hopefully, we have the right family," I say, crossing my fingers.

Tom shakes me. "You did it, Carrie. I think you did it."

Everybody starts talking at once. But then Lisa says, "So now what? When will you know for sure?"

"He should be calling anytime now."

"But what if this Christine messes up the story and he doesn't want to talk to you? People at the store are always miscommunicating."

"Yeah," says Molly. "And if this James Mitchell is the right one, why hasn't he called?"

They're right. Why isn't the phone ringing?

"You two are terrible," Tom says. "How many families in Seattle have three James Mitchells?" *Ring. Ring.*

"See?" Tom says, thumbing his nose at L and M.

My body freezes. "You get it," I say, pointing to Tom. *Ring.* Tom shakes his head. *Ring.* Lisa pushes me toward the phone. "What if he's the wrong one?"

"Hurry up," Molly says. "They're going to hang up."

"Hello, O'Learys . . . This is Carrie O'Leary . . . Oh, Mr. Mitchell, I'm so happy to hear from you . . . You did have a father who served in World War II on the Aleutian Chain . . . around 1942 or 1943? When did he die? . . . Oh, wonderful, I mean I'm sorry. . . ."

When I finally hang up, they all run up to me, screaming. "Is it him?"

"Yes. His dad died in the battle of Attu just like Uncle Billy wrote in the letter. He was only one, and his dad never got to see him. He wants to drive over as soon as possible to meet me and get his letter. And he apologized for taking so long to call back, but he wanted to verify the Well Street address with his mother."

"So when is he going to come?" Molly asks excitedly.

"I told him I'd have to call him back because of Gram and everything."

Just then Mom pokes her head into the kitchen. "Come on, kids. Your grandmother wants to see you."

My heart starts pounding for the second time this morning. "What, Mother?" Aunt Rosemary is saying as we walk in. Gram closes her eyes, then opens them again quickly. She looks up at all of us crowded around her bed and holds out her hands. "Hello, dears."

I can hardly stand to look at Gram until I realize she's smiling, her beautiful smile. One by one we hug her. I'm last. When I stand up, I look at her face, and one lone tear has slipped out of her eye and rolled down her cheek. Then she closes her eyes and never opens them again.

Chapter Eighteen

WE ALL JUST STAND THERE, looking at Gram. Tears start coming down my face. I don't even try to wipe them away. She is out of pain now. She is with God and Gramps and Uncle Billy. But she is not with us.

Finally Dad motions us into the living room. Everybody's crying and hugging. Dad leaves to call Father McCann and the funeral home.

Mom says, "Why don't we fix a nice breakfast? I can make a fruit salad and eggs. We have some fruit, don't we, Lisa?" Lisa nods. "We can talk about Ann and all the good times. She would want that."

"How can you think about food at a time like this?" I say, running back into Gram's room, but stopping suddenly. Her body is lying perfectly still, and the locket around her neck isn't moving. There's no blood going through her veins and no color in her cheeks, but she has such a peaceful look on her face.

I can't bear to touch her. "Gram, I love you. I'll never forget you." I'm crying so hard that I don't hear Mom come in.

"Carrie, your grandmother wanted you to have her locket. Why don't we take it off her now?"

"No, Mom. We can't."

"Yes, help me." We gently prop Gram up on the pillows, and Mom takes the necklace off Gram and puts it around my neck. I stand there, watching Gram and gripping the locket until the men from the funeral home show up.

I don't want to stay, but Molly is digging her nails into me like she'll never let go. It reminds me of the day when Gram broke her hip and was taken away in an ambulance, except this time Gram won't be coming home.

When the big black funeral car finally leaves, Mom gets us to come into the kitchen and fix breakfast. When Father McCann arrives, Dad and Aunt Rosemary talk to him in the living room about the funeral arrangements. I don't feel like eating, but when I finally do, I realize I'm hungry.

In the middle of the meal, Molly suddenly says, "Tell Mom your news, Carrie."

"Not now, Molly."

"Tell me, honey. We all could use some happy news."

"Go on." Tom nudges me. I haven't even thought about the letter since we got called into Gram's bedroom. Then it hits me.

"Oh, no. After all that, I didn't even get a chance to tell Gram I found James Mitchell."

"You found him, Carrie? How wonderful." Mom comes over and hugs me.

"Yeah, and now Mr. Mitchell wants to come over to meet her and get the letter." Molly can't hold back even today. But I'm not mad. "I bet he even gives you a reward."

"Mom, he shouldn't come with Gram just—"

"Honey, we'll work something out. Your grandmother would be so proud of you. She smiled when she hugged you this morning. I think she knew in her heart that you had found him."

"But I never got to tell her." I start crying again.

Mom looks around at everybody. "Didn't Gram have a way of knowing things you didn't even tell her? And she loved us each in a very special way. How I'm going to miss her." Now my mom is crying.

Later, I overhear Molly talking to Mom. "So can he come over soon? He must be dying to get that letter."

"We'll have to talk to your father. There's so much to decide right now, with Gram's funeral and all."

"Molly, stop bugging Mom. It's okay if it has to wait. I wanted to find the owner before Gram died, and in a way I did. But Gram's funeral is most important now."

When Dad and Aunt Rosemary finally sit down to eat, they ask us what we think Gram would like at her funeral mass. Lisa suggests some of Gram's favorite church songs, and Tom thinks we should have a potluck afterward with all of Gram's favorite foods.

Suddenly Mom remembers it's Sunday, so we all decide to go to noon mass and pray for Gram. But I can't pray. All I can think about are the special times I shared with Gram when she wasn't sick. Afterward Dad says he and Aunt Rosemary are going to the funeral home as soon as Mom and Lisa pick out one of Gram's dresses. Aunt Rosemary wants Tom to go, but I don't want to. I'd like to see Gram one last time in private and tell her about the letter. But I don't want to look at her in the casket. I'm going to be cremated when I die.

The rest of the day the house is filled with people and food. Tonight, after Dad has called all the out-of-town relatives, I can hear my parents talking in the kitchen.

"I know this is hard, Will. I'm so sorry your mother died." Then their voices lower, and I can't hear what they're saying until Dad says, "You're right. Of course you're right. Mr. Mitchell should come a day or two after the funeral while Tom and Rosemary are still here. I guess I should look at it as another way of honoring my mother and Uncle Billy."

Later, when I call James Mitchell, I'm so excited I can hardly talk. But I also feel guilty, like I shouldn't be happy on the same day Gram dies. It's all so confusing. I wish Gram were going to be here to hand the letter over to James Mitchell.

After a few minutes of stumbling around trying to explain things to him, I'm relieved when Mom takes the phone. She tells JM II about some nearby motels and says that anytime Thursday or Friday would work out well for us.

Mom gets off the phone and keeps saying, "It will be fine, Carrie. Just fine." Who is she trying to convince? "You girls can make a cake and we'll have lemonade and it will be fine. Such a roller coaster of emotions, lately, huh?" Then she hugs me again hard.

Today there are even more visitors and food—salads, casseroles, breads, desserts. I've never seen so much food in this house at one time. It seems like everyone Gram ever knew drops by, wanting to tell us how much they cared about her.

This afternoon I go with Dad to Holy Cross Cemetery to see Gram's gravesite. It's right next to Gramps's under a tree at the top of the hill. We stand for a long time looking at his gravestone—Patrick Robert O'Leary. It's raining hard, but we don't care.

It's hard to believe that only two months ago Gram and I planted poppies here, and now they're blooming brightly. Things can change so fast.

I stare at the grassy part next to Gramps's grave. Soon it will have Gram's marker—Ann Marie Sweeney O'Leary. They haven't started digging it up yet. So until she's in the ground, I guess I can still pretend she's alive. But who am I kidding?

On the way home Dad says, "I'm very proud of you, Carrie, for finding James Mitchell."

"Thanks, Dad. But now I'm kind of scared."

"Scared? To meet Mr. Mitchell?"

"No, to give the letter up. In a way, it was part of Gram, too, and when it's gone . . ."

"You really did it for her, didn't you?"

"Yes, in the beginning. But I did it for me, too, and the Mitchells. I loved doing the search. It gave me something to do besides worry about Gram." I look out the window and trace my name in the wet moisture. "At least we still have Gram and Uncle Billy's letters."

"Yes, we do, and we can look at them whenever we want."

"Dad, what if the letter upsets Mr. Mitchell?"

"It's out of your hands now, Carrie. We can't control his reaction. People deal with things in different ways."

"Like some people falling apart when someone dies and others not even shedding a tear?"

Mr. Kingston was out of town when Gram died yesterday, but he comes over tonight the minute he gets back. It's so good to see him. I talk about Gram and then in the middle of telling him about how I located James Mitchell, Jr., I suddenly realize I've never told Mad. How could I be so selfish? I yell at Molly to tell Mr. K the rest of the story, and I tear out of the house.

Running over to Mad's, I realize that I haven't seen her at all since I got back from Seattle. She doesn't even known that Gram's dead. Where has she been?

When I get there, nobody's home and their car is gone. Yesterday's and today's papers are still on the front porch. I go home and call, and all I get is the message machine.

Are they out of town? But they never go anywhere. I have to tell Mad about James Mitchell. She's going to be so excited. What if she misses Gram's funeral? She'll be upset. Where could she have gone?

This morning Mad's still not home. So I get the idea to call the art gallery where her mom works. At first they don't want to tell me if Patty Connors is on vacation, but when I give them the whole story about Gram, they relent and put me through to the manager. She tells me that Patty took a couple of days off, but that if she hears from her, she'll be sure and tell her about Ann O'Leary.

This day is really dragging by. All I can think about is the rosary tonight, wondering if I'll break down in front of everyone. Then I remember this letter of Gram's that I've been wanting to reread. When I find it, I go out on the patio where Molly, Lisa, and Tom are sitting around.

"Can I read you guys a letter?" They nod. "It means something different to me now."

October 4, 1945

Dear Billy,

For two years now we've had a gold star in our window. You can almost see people bow their heads when they walk by. But somehow that doesn't make it any easier. Once last year in the *Chronicle* there was a picture of a woman who had already lost three sons in the war and now was saying good-bye to her youngest, who had just joined the army.

She looked so strong. Why can't I be? I know how cruel Hitler and the Japanese have been, but a part of me wishes that you had never gone to war.

On V-J Day I got caught up in the celebration on Market Street for a while, especially when I saw a cute soldier with dark, curly hair wearing army green. For one fleeting second I thought it was you, home early to surprise us. Then I remembered that you would never be coming home.

I sometimes wonder how you died and what it's like in heaven. Are you looking down, dear brother, and watching over us?

Dad doesn't talk much anymore. Mother kept busy wrapping bandages and knitting socks during the war, but now that it's over, she doesn't know what to do. Neither do I. I have an office job, but what I really want to do is go to college. Mother just wants me to meet a good man and get married. So many soldiers back home now to date. I guess I should consider some of the offers.

I miss you so much, Billy, and I will never, ever forget you. Someday I hope to be with you in heaven.

Love,
Annie

"Wow," Lisa says. Nobody speaks for a minute.

Then Molly says, "I'm never going to forget Gram, just like she never forgot her brother."

We sit around playing hearts because that was Gram's favorite card game. But after a few games, we all get depressed again. Molly starts jiggling her lawn chair, driving us all crazy, until finally Lisa says, "Maybe you should go take a swim, Molly."

"I can't do that. Not on the day of Gram's rosary."

"Of course you can. Gram doesn't want your life to stop because she died. Go swim for Gram. It'll help you get through tomorrow."

"Okay, you're the boss." And before we know it, Molly has grabbed her swim bag and is gone.

Tom, Lisa, and I look at one another as if to say, Well, what do we do to get through all this? Just then Mom comes outside with Nancy and Becky, of all people.

"Hi. We were sorry to hear about your grandma. So my mom said we should come over and visit because that's what people do when someone dies."

I'm so startled to see them that I don't say anything until Lisa nudges me. "Uh, hi, Becky. Thanks, Nancy." I'm actually flattered they've come until I catch Nancy looking at Tom. Is that why they're here?

"Your mom said it would be all right if you went for ice cream with us."

"Oh, I don't know. All these people are here. And . . . Oh, yeah. Becky and Nancy, this is my cousin Tom."

"Hi," Tom says quietly. I check to see if Nancy's flirting, but she's not.

She does say, "Oh, Tom, you should come along, and you, too, Lisa."

Tom says, "Thanks, but I'd better stay here with my mother." And Lisa shakes her head.

I start to shake my head, too, but both Tom and Lisa say, "Go," and practically push me off the patio. I wish I knew why they'd come over.

"Great," Nancy says. "Get your bike and meet us out front."

Tom goes inside and I turn to Lisa. "I don't trust them."

"Oh, just have some fun for once."

"All right. But if Madeline shows up, tell her I won't be gone long."

"Okay. Okay. Now go."

Biking along, I suddenly feel this big release. I'm alive, able to go for ice cream and bike wherever I want. Gram won't ever eat ice cream again. Father McCann says heaven's even better. But what if he's wrong?

I keep expecting Nancy to ask about Tom, but she doesn't bring him up until we're waiting to order our cones at the ice cream parlor. "Your cousin's cute." I smile but don't say anything.

On the way home, in front of Northtown Shopping Center we see this bear dressed in a tuxedo waving at all the cars.

"That's my date to the junior prom," Becky yells out.

"He does look kind of cute," I say.

"I'll be lucky if I have even *him* for a date." Right, Nancy, I think. You're just fishing for compliments, and I'm not going to give you the pleasure.

"But I'll bet he's pretty sweaty under there. What if he wants to bear hug all night?" Finally Nancy has something funny to say.

We all start laughing so hard that I think I'm going to wet

my pants. We turn onto a side street and get off our bikes, falling onto the grass in somebody's yard. It feels so good to lie on the cool, green carpet. I keep laughing and laughing until suddenly I'm not laughing anymore; I'm crying.

"Are you okay, Carrie?" Becky asks.

"I don't know. It's like I feel guilty for having fun when my gram just died."

"But I know she wants you to be happy, Carrie." I turn and look at Nancy. Sometimes she's all right.

When Becky and Nancy drop me off, Madeline is waiting in our front yard. I jump off my bike and run over and hug her. Everybody's startled, including me. "Ah, Mad's been gone for a few days. I missed her."

"I guess so. Hello, Madeline," Nancy says.

"Yeah, hi."

"Thanks for the ice cream, you guys."

"Sure. Hope the funeral goes all right, Carrie."

"Thanks, Nancy."

"See you later," Becky yells out as they bike down the street.

"What was that all about?" Mad says, looking me over.

"I don't know. They just showed up. Feeling sorry for me, I guess."

"Yeah, I'm really sorry about your gram. She was one fine lady." Mad has tears in her eyes.

"Yes, she was." Then I look at Mad hard. "Where have you been? I left you billions of messages."

"I know. Thanks for calling Mom's work to let them know about your gram. I would have been really bummed out if I'd missed her funeral."

"So where did you go?"

"To see my dad."

"What?" I sit down on the porch steps. "How did that happen?"

Mad sits down beside me. "Well, I was ticked off the day

you left for Seattle. Here you've got all this family and I've got nobody except Mom. So I told her I was taking off to find my dad. I thought of just running away, but—"

"Oh, I'm glad you didn't. Your mother would have been so worried."

"Well, she didn't believe me at first, but then I started crying and screaming, and it finally sunk in, especially when I said I was going to hitchhike. So she called my dad and told him his daughter wanted to meet him. It turns out she's known where he was all along but thought it was up to him to contact me first."

"So what happened?"

"Well, he lives in Wallace, Idaho, only a hundred miles from here, and he said he'd be happy to meet me. So Mom took a couple of days off work and drove me over there." Mad picks up a blade of grass and starts chewing on it.

"What's he like?" I feel like I'm screaming at her, but she's so calm.

"He's okay."

"Okay? The first time you meet your dad and you call him okay?"

"Well, he's fat like me and drinks too much. But he's not alcoholic. His house is messy, but it's got lots of books and records. I think he liked seeing me. I mean he didn't really know how to talk to me, and I didn't know what to say to him. But . . ."

"Are you going to see him again?"

"Probably. Maybe I'll even live with him sometime if my mom drives me nutty."

"What's he do?"

"He's a miner."

"A rich gold miner?"

"No, more like a poor silver miner."

"Oh . . . Well, is he married?" Geez, did I have to pull everything out of her?

"Nope. Not after my mom. Said he wasn't the type for commitment."

I can't tell if Mad's happy she met her dad or not, but at least she has one now.

It's not until Mad's leaving that I remember to tell her about the lost letter. She gets really excited, much more than about her dad. Are those other feelings too close to the heart to share? I tell Mad I want her to be here when James Mitchell, Jr., comes, and she says, "Of course."

Later I go to my room, take out a piece of paper, and start writing.

Gram's funeral mass was beautiful. I cried a little, but mostly I tried to think about all the good times we'd had together and all the things she'd said to me over the years. I tried to freeze in my mind an image of Gram when she was healthy and alive.

Father McCann talked about what a strong woman Gram was and how she rarely complained about the pain and other sorrows in her life. Tom got up and read one of Gram's favorite Emily Dickinson poems. And Dad spoke a few words for the family, thanking everyone for all they'd done for Gram and us. Neither of them cracked. I could never be so poised. We said the Irish blessing, "May the Road Rise To Meet You, and ended with one of Gram's favorite songs, "Amazing Grace." Grace. That's what Gram always said got her through.

Tonight Dad told us that Gram set up what money she had left in college funds for all the grandchildren and also put aside some money for both families to take a trip to San Francisco. Now I'll be able to visit Uncle Billy's grave and maybe even the house where Gram grew up with Uncle Billy and her dolls. But it won't be the same as going with her. Dad said she also asked that the letters and dolls be kept in her father's trunk and available for any family member to look at whenever they wanted.

I'm sad as I lie in bed tonight, touching Gram's locket. I'll never take that dream trip with her. I'll never sit and hear her stories again. My only consolation is that tomorrow Mr. Mitchell finally gets his letter.

Chapter Nineteen

I WAKE UP EARLY and pull the letter out from under my pillow. I study it one last time, not sure whether I'm ready to give it up or not.

Then it hits me. We've all been so sad about Gram and counting on meeting the Mitchells to cheer us up. But James Mitchell III died just two months ago, and he never even knew this grandfather who wrote the letter. What if today only makes James Mitchell sadder?

We all help clean the house, and then Molly and Lisa make the lemonade and set the table while Tom and I decorate the cake. I'm so glad Aunt Rosemary said they could stay through the weekend.

But now it's only one-thirty. Another whole hour to wait. We start another game of hearts, but I keep looking out the window every few minutes, worried they might be lost. At two o'clock the doorbell rings. I jump up and run to the door.

"Mad." She looks nice, wearing an embroidered denim shirt and jeans.

"I know I'm not 'the guy,' but couldn't you at least fake it?"

"Stop it. You look great. This never would have happened without you, you know."

"Would too. You were so determined. Nothing would have stopped you."

"But you deserve at least half the credit."

"It was fun. I kinda miss doing it."

"So do I."

We sit on the front porch steps, and I finally give her the blow-by-blow account of my trip to Seattle and the phone calls to Christine and James Mitchell, Jr. She doesn't interrupt me once.

Then, out of the blue, she jumps up. "Look at that car cruising up and down, checking addresses. That must be them."

"It can't be. There's so many people in the car." But then they stop in front and my family comes pouring out of the house and Mr. Kingston and Patty Connors come walking down the street.

By the time I get myself down to the car, this handsome man, a little older than Dad, with salt-and-pepper hair and blue eyes, is shaking my hand. "Carrie, what a pleasure. I can't tell you how grateful I am. This is my wife, Kathy, and my daughter-in-law, Christine." Then he helps an older woman out of the car. "And this is my mother, Dorothy."

I feel like I've been knocked over with a bowling pin. Mr. Mitchell mentioned his mother, but it never really clicked that James Mitchell, Sr.'s wife was actually still alive. I'm trembling when I take her hand, but then I relax because it's almost like shaking Gram's hand.

Dad tries to introduce everybody, but it gets all jumbled up, so Mom suggests we go into the house.

On the way in, I whisper to my dad, "What do I do now? Just hand him the letter? I didn't think about this part, only about finding him."

"I think it should be more formal than that. When we all get seated in the living room, you can give it to him."

In all the commotion I'd forgotten to bring the letter with me, so I rush into my bedroom to get it. But when I pick it up, I start crying. I slowly walk back to the living room, trying to brush away the tears. When I enter, the conversation stops.

"Mr. Mitchell, here's the lost letter. I hope it's as special to you as it has been to me." He stands up and carefully takes it from my hand.

"Carrie, I don't know how to thank you." Then, without even sitting down, he takes out his Swiss army knife and opens the letter. I wasn't sure he was going to do it in front of us. But I'm happy he does. Maybe he knows that he can trust us.

As he silently reads the letter, tears start coming down his face. But when he finishes, he's smiling.

"Though we've just met, I feel connected to your family in a special way, so I'd like to share my father's letter with you all." He goes over and hugs his mother and then starts reading.

May 24, 1943

Dear Son,

It's hard to believe that soon you'll be one year old and yet it looks like now we'll never meet on this earth. I love you, son, so very much, and just because I've never laid eyes on you doesn't change that one bit.

And I love your mother. She's beautiful and strong and I want you to take care of her for me. I know she'll take good care of you.

I wish I could hang on, Jimmy, but I've lost too much blood. Doc here is taking care of me the best he can, and he's promised to deliver this letter to you and your mother in person. I'm not afraid to die, son. I just wish that I could have seen you at least once.

It's quite a place here. Rains and williwaws every day even though it's May. But then in the evening there'll be a brilliant sunset—like right now.

Little Jimmy, I have to believe that our being here, fighting this war, is important. In a year I've had such a mixture of feelings of fear and jubilance, suffering and comradeship.

War is awful. Yet I honestly feel grateful for being a participant in a very small way in such a world event. We're trying to get the island of Attu back from the Japanese. It's American territory and there's no telling what the Japanese will do next if they take over the entire Chain.

Give Grandma and your mother a hug, Jimmy. Don't ever forget how much I love you. Work and play hard and love others and yourself. All the rest will follow. I know I'll always be proud of you.

Love,
Dad

The room is silent for a moment, and then Mr. Mitchell comes over and gives me a hug. "Thank you, Carrie, for this incredible gift. To get a letter from my father after all these years means so much, especially now that I've had a son of my own." He starts to choke but catches himself.

Mr. Mitchell passes around a photo of him and his mother. He was so cute as a baby, and Mrs. Mitchell was really pretty with her hair up. She's still pretty.

"I fought in Vietnam, so I know some of what my dad went through. I guess I was the lucky one. How I wish I could have known him. But at least I knew my son."

Mrs. Dorothy Mitchell smiles when the photograph reaches her. It seems like everybody is wiping away tears now.

"But we have so much to live for," Mr. Mitchell says, looking around at his family and then us. "And you, young lady, are amazing. Sounds like you just wouldn't give up. They probably don't know what to do with you in school, you're so smart." I expect one of my sisters to laugh, but neither one does.

"I couldn't have done it without everyone's help." I want to say more, but my mouth just won't move.

Mom stands up and saves me. "Mr. Mitchell, our young people made a special cake to commemorate this event." She motions us all over to the dining room table. "Carrie, why don't you read it out loud?" I shake my head and point to Madeline.

"World War II—James Mitchell, Sr. Billy Sweeney—Memories."

Everyone claps. "Mr. Mitchell," I hear myself say, "would you cut the first piece?"

"How about if my mother does the honors?" I nod happily as Dorothy Mitchell takes the knife from my mom.

Tom and Madeline help pass out the cake, and Molly and Lisa serve the lemonade. Then Mr. Mitchell makes a toast. "To Carrie Ann O'Leary—detective extraordinaire." Everybody cheers. "And to our loved ones who have passed on and all those who have died defending our country."

"May I make a toast, Mr. Mitchell?" I ask. He smiles at me. "To my friend Madeline, who kept me going; Mr. Kingston, who always listened; my cousin Tom, who always makes me feel better; to my parents, who love me; and my two sisters, who put up with me no matter what." Everybody cheers again.

Then, just as I'm about to bite into my cake, Mr. Mitchell speaks again. "One more thing. I have something special here for Carrie." He hands me an envelope. "Go ahead. Open it up." I take out the piece of paper. A savings bond for two hundred and fifty dollars. Madeline whistles.

"Mr. Mitchell . . ." My dad starts to protest.

"No, no. A letter from my father is worth every penny of that and more. It's the least I could do. It will mature when Carrie is about ready to start college. And anybody as smart as she is deserves a little help with her education. She'll probably end up as a detective, a reporter, a lawyer. Something snoopy like that." Everybody laughs, and I start turning red.

Finally when things settle down, Mr. Mitchell motions me over to two empty chairs. "Now I want you to tell me every last detail about how you found me."

I tell him about the phone calls and sending out all the

letters and getting the negative ones back. Then when Mr. K joins us, we start talking about the war on the Aleutians. Mr. Mitchell has done some reading, but he still asks Mr. K a lot of questions. It's fun to trade information.

"What did happen to your great-uncle?"

"He died at Kiska, a month later."

"But I thought there was no fighting there. That the Japanese snuck out in the fog during the night."

"I know," I say. "He died in friendly fire. I think that's what made Billy's death so hard for Gram—that it could have been avoided."

Mr. Mitchell shakes his head and starts talking about his son Jimmy's motorcycle accident. Then I tell him about Gram's cancer.

I don't notice the time until I look around the room and realize that everybody else is gone. Mom's out in the kitchen talking with Mr. Mitchell's wife, Kathy, and Dorothy Mitchell is telling a joke to the rest of them on the patio.

When we join them, Mr. Mitchell makes another announcement. "Billy Sweeney took care of my father in his dying moments. In honor of both of them, I would like to take you all out to dinner."

Mom hesitates and then says, "Thanks, Jim. But it's been quite stressful these last few days, so I think—"

"You know, Susan," my dad says, interrupting, "why don't we go? I think it's just what the doctor ordered."

Everybody decides to come, even Mr. K, Madeline, and her mother. On the way out to the car, I remember something I want to bring.

At dinner we laugh and talk as if we've known one another for a long time. I can't stop munching on tortilla chips. Finally Mad leans over and whispers, "Slow down, wudja? There *is* a tomorrow." I look around, embarrassed. I feel like I haven't eaten in days.

When the waiter comes into our private dining room to take dessert orders, I decide to skip it. There's something else

I want to do instead. But I'm still not sure. So I whisper to Dorothy Mitchell, and she squeezes my arm. "Yes."

I tap my knife on the water glass to get everyone's attention. "You could say that I've lived with letters all summer. Through them I got to know my Uncle Billy and my grandmother better. Fifty years ago, Gram wrote Uncle Billy a letter after he died. Yesterday I decided to write Gram one, since I never really got to say good-bye to her the way I wanted to."

I take a sip of water and go on. "And since Mr. Mitchell was so generous to read his father's letter aloud today, I'd like to read mine to Gram." My voice starts to shake, but Dorothy Mitchell pats my hand. And once I start speaking, I'm fine.

July 26

Dear Gram,

I miss you so much already. You were so brave through your illness. Will I be that strong when my time comes? Help me, okay?

I found the owner of the lost letter, Gram. Can you believe it? Right before you died. I'll bet you even heard us screaming about it in the kitchen. But now you're in heaven with Uncle Billy and Gramps and you've probably already met Jimmy Mitchell. We're going to meet his son after your funeral.

Today I sat in your old room, but I can't bear the thought of moving back in yet. I want it to be your place for a while. Mom said I could take my time and then Molly offered to move in there instead, so I could stay in her old room. Isn't that nice, Gram? I hate to say this, but I think your sickness and dying brought the rest of us closer. Why does it have to be that way? Why couldn't we just do it on our own?

I'm still confused about why you didn't talk about Uncle Billy, Gram. How can you love somebody that much and not talk about him? But Dad said it was your right to do whatever you had to do to get through the pain. I'm just glad I found those letters because it helped all of us to know you better. We're going to talk about you, Gram. We're not going to forget you.

My tears are dripping on this paper, Gram. When does that go away? You told me once that you fill up the hole with other people. All right, but I want a little bit of a hole left, just so I don't ever forget you. I'm glad you aren't in pain anymore, Gram. But I sure wish you didn't have to die. Please look down on us every day.

Love,
Your granddaughter Carrie Ann

P.S. I can't wait to give James Mitchell, Junior, the letter. I hope he's as happy with it as I was about finding him. So many people helped me, Gram, just like they helped you. And, Gram, Uncle Billy *was* a hero. He helped Jimmy Mitchell die with dignity.

When I finish, my dad comes and hugs me and then the desserts arrive, but nobody wants them anymore. It just feels like it's time to leave—time to get some fresh air stirred in with all the emotions of the past week.

When we leave the restaurant, I hug Dorothy Mitchell and she says, "You stay in touch, Carrie, dear. And when you come to Seattle, you must look us up."

Mr. Mitchell shakes everybody's hand and then takes me by the shoulders. "You are a very determined young woman. Don't you ever lose that."

Chapter Twenty

EARLY THE NEXT MORNING the phone rings, and Molly answers it. Then she rouses me out of bed, yelling, "Carrie, Carrie, wake up. It's the *Spokesman-Review*. They want to talk to you."

The newspaper? It turns out they want to run an article about how I tracked down James Mitchell and made it a special mission for my dying grandmother. They also want to know if Mr. Mitchell is still in town so they can take a picture with me.

I get off the phone and right away call his motel. They haven't checked out, and Mr. Mitchell says he would be honored to pose for a photo with me.

So thirty minutes later I'm sitting in the living room with the Mitchells again and Tom and my sisters and even Madeline (I went over and banged on her door until she woke up), waiting for the newspaper photographer and reporter. And then Mr. Kingston shows up. First they interview Mr. Mitchell and me and then start taking photos. I tell the reporter how everybody else helped, too, but she says they want a photo of just the two of us.

The next day when the article runs, it's like the day Gram died, except nobody brings food and it's a much happier time. The phone keeps ringing. Nancy and Becky show up again, and one call is from Ms. Chambers, my old social studies teacher. I don't know what to say, but luckily Ms. Chambers does all the talking.

When I hang up, I scream, "Ms. Chambers is going to teach eighth-grade social studies next year!"

"What?" Mad says, walking into the kitchen.

Then I tell all three of them how she wants me to bring

in Uncle Billy's war letters and tell the class all about World War II in Alaska.

"That's terrible," Mad said. Then she sees my face. "I mean not about the letters, about her being our teacher again." Then she stops a minute. "Well, maybe not. At least I'll know what to expect."

"Maybe this presentation will help me get off to a better start," I say.

"I guess I could do better, too. Except Mother says that all I care about is boys and that Ms. Chambers knows it."

"Well, isn't it, Nancy?" Mad says, laughing. Becky and I join in.

Nancy frowns, but then the doorbell rings again. Lisa comes marching into the kitchen with this smirky look on her face. "Carrie, you have more visitors."

"Joe . . . Leon . . ." I can feel my face turning bright pink.

"Hi, we decided to come by and congratulate the famous detective in person."

"Ah . . . thanks."

"Oh . . . hi, Becky, Nancy. Hi, Madeline. Didn't see you guys sitting there," Leon says, chomping on gum.

Nobody says anything for a minute, not even Mad, and then Tom comes slamming in the back door and just looks at everybody.

Finally Lisa says, "Carrie, aren't you going to introduce Tom?"

"Oh, yeah. Joe, Leon, this is my cousin Tom from Seattle."

They say hi and then everybody just looks at one another again. Until Mad whispers something in Becky's ear and they start laughing. Lisa shrugs her shoulders and leaves the room, as if to say, Carrie, you're on your own now. Finally Tom suggests some lemonade and I say yes, very loudly, and get out the glasses so Tom can pour it.

We all just sit around talking about the letter for a few minutes, and then Nancy says she has to get home, and

Becky, Joe, and Leon decide to leave, too. Why did they come over? Because Nancy and Becky were here? Everything's so confusing.

Later at, dinner, the whole family sits around eating leftovers from Gram's potluck. Giggling, Lisa asks how my day was and then whispers in Molly's ear, and they both start laughing.

After dinner, Tom and I sit on the patio while the others clean up. He mentions that Joe and Leon seem like nice guys, and I say that they're okay. Then I blurt out to Tom that he's the only brother I'll ever have and that I hope we can always be friends until we're as old as Gram.

I feel like I'm going to cry again. But I don't. I just sit there instead, not talking. A big part of me wants to go back to when Gram was alive and Sally lived behind us and I was smart in school. But I can't.

So I guess I'll just have to wait and see what the future holds. Will I be a detective or lawyer like Mr. Mitchell says? Maybe I'll be a reporter. I guess I could start by working on being a gold star person. That seems like the hardest job of all.

That's what Gram was—a gold star person. She told me once that when she died, she'd be my guardian angel. How will I recognize her? By the gold star on her wings?

ABOUT THE AUTHOR

Claire Rudolf Murphy, a native of Spokane, Washington, has spent much of her life exploring the Pacific Northwest and Alaska. Ms. Murphy's previous books include *The Prince and the Salmon People*; *To the Summit*; and *Friendship Across Arctic Waters: Alaskan Cub Scouts Visit Their Soviet Neighbors*. She lives in Fairbanks, Alaska.